THE GUNSMITH

481

Cheap Whiskey and Sad Women

Books by J.R. Roberts
(Robert J. Randisi)

The Gunsmith series

Gunsmith Giant series

Lady Gunsmith series

Angel Eyes series

Tracker series

Mountain Jack Pike series

COMING SOON!
The Gunsmith
482 – Chanteuse from the East

For more information
visit: www.SpeakingVolumes.us

THE GUNSMITH

481

Cheap Whiskey and Sad Women

J. R. Roberts

SPEAKING VOLUMES, LLC
NAPLES, FLORIDA
2023

Cheap Whiskey and Sad Women

ISBN 978-1-64540-915-1

Chapter One

Louisville, Kentucky

One of the first things Clint Adams learned about Louisville, Kentucky was that, despite how it was spelled, it was pronounced "Loo-ville." He heard that his first night in The Shamrock Saloon where he was supposed to meet his friend, Bat Masterson.

Bat had contacted Clint and asked him to meet him there. He had given no indication of why, but they were good enough friends for Clint to come anyway. He assumed Bat had a good reason. All he had made clear was that he wanted Clint to meet him in The Shamrock Saloon.

When Clint entered, it was afternoon. Most of the tables were empty, and none of the occupied ones had Bat Masterson seated at them.

There were a few men at the bar, and Clint joined them there.

"What kin I getcha?" the bartender asked.

"Beer."

"Yer in Kentucky, friend," the man said. "Sure you don't want some bourbon?"

"Beer will do for now."

"Comin' up."

While the bartender brought Clint his beer, the other men looked him over.

"Got somethin' against bourbon?" a man further down the bar asked.

"Not really," Clint replied, "I just prefer beer."

"Nothin' wrong with that," the bartender said, loudly, looking to head off any trouble, "is there?"

"Hell, no!" another man shouted. "Let the man drink what he wants."

Clint lifted his glass in a salute to the man, turned and did the same to the bartender. Then he sipped his beer and leaned on the bar.

"You just get to town?" the bartender asked.

"About an hour ago," Clint said. "Got myself and my horse settled, then decided on a beer. After this I'll be looking for a meal."

"You might want to try across the street," the bartender said. "Cousin Louie's Café. Good food."

"And bourbon?" Clint asked.

The bartender laughed and said, "And fine beer."

"And what's your connection?" Clint asked.

"You think I'm gettin' a kickback?"

"Could be."

"What's it matter if the food's good?"

"Good point," Clint said. "I'll give it a try."

"Can I help you with anythin' else?"

Clint had decided not to ask anyone if they had seen Bat Masterson or describe his friend. He and Bat would know each other on sight, and that was good enough. If Bat didn't show up, there would be time to ask questions then.

He finished his beer and started for the door.

"Tell Cousin Louie I said hi," the bartender called.

"I'll do that."

***

Cousin Louie's was a small, well-furnished café, with both a waiter and a waitress working the floor. There was a good lunch crowd, and since the front window afforded a nice view of the street, people liked to sit there. So there was no problem for Clint to get a back table.

"Good-afternoon, sir," the pretty waitress greeted. "Welcome to Louie's."

Clint had scanned the room quickly and found no sign of Bat. He assumed he had arrived in town before his friend.

"I'll start with coffee," Clint said, "but I'll need a suggestion from you about what to eat."

"That won't be a problem," she said. "We have several dishes that we are known for."

"Nothing cooked with bourbon, I hope."

"We have one very good one," she said, "but I won't serve it to you."

"Fine but otherwise, surprise me."

"I will."

She came back with a pot of coffee for him, which was no surprise, but that changed when she brought his meal. She set a bowl in front of him and waited for his reaction.

"What have we here?" he asked.

"It's Burgoo," she said.

"It looks like a stew."

"It's very much like stew, but rather than prepared with beef it sometimes features, squirrel, possum or raccoon."

Clint peered into the bowl.

"Which is this?"

"Restaurants sometimes use their own recipe. We make it with pork."

"It smells great. Do I see potatoes?"

"Potatoes, cabbage, lima beans and tomatoes," the waitress said. "It's all used as a thickener. It keeps the Burgoo from comin' out soupy. Enjoy. I have other tables, but I'll check back with you. My name is Jane."

She hurried away before he could thank her.

4

Chapter Two

Clint found the Burgoo delicious and somewhat spicy. Lisa brought him another pot of coffee and asked, "How is it?"

"Very good," Clint said. "I've never had vegetables cooked better."

"Would you like a second bowl?"

"Very much."

She smiled as she took his bowl and said, "I love a man with a big appetite."

He smiled at her, and she went to the kitchen then brought him a second helping of Burgoo and bread.

As it moved into late afternoon the place filled with more customers. Clint finished his second bowl of Burgoo and was too full for a piece of pie.

"Come back later, when it's not so busy," Lisa said, "I'll save a piece for you. Rhubarb?"

"Oh, no," Clint said, with distaste. "Anything but that."

"Cherry?"

"Perfect," he said, paying his check. "I'll see you later."

"I look forward to it."

He got a sour look from several young men, as well as the waiter. The waitress seemed to be very popular among the young males.

Clint decided to spend the rest of the day and evening in the Shamrock. There was no point in walking around town to look for Bat. The Shamrock was the chosen meeting place. Bat would be there either this night or the next, unless something had happened.

As it got dark outside, two girls, brunette and blonde, in frilly dresses came down the stairs and started working the floor. Two dealers also appeared and took position at a Faro and blackjack table. Clint stayed away from both games and sat at a back table nursing his beer.

"Another cold one?" the brunette asked him.

"Why not?" he said, pushing the warm, last half of one towards her.

She picked it up and said, "You're wasting a lot of good beer."

"You're right," he said, "but I'm just killing time."

"Waitin' for a friend? Or a girl?"

"A friend."

"Well," she said, "maybe that's good news for Barbara or me."

She went to the bar and came back with a cold beer.

"Let me know if you need anything else," she said. "Anything. My name is Lisa."

As the girl flounced away Clint sipped his beer and kept his eyes on the batwing doors.

***

While bringing him another beer and removing the next warm half, Lisa told him that the saloons in town closed at midnight.

"Do you have a room?" she asked.

"Yes, I do, in a hotel not far from here."

"The Bluegrass?"

"That's the one."

"It's a nice place," she told him.

"How does the food compare to the café across the street?" he asked.

"Louie's? That's the best, but the Bluegrass isn't bad for breakfast."

"That's good to know."

She looked around, didn't see anyone trying to get her attention, so she sat across from him.

"What will you do if your friend doesn't show up tonight?" she asked.

"I'll come back and wait tomorrow. He'll be here eventually."

"You're sure?"

"Positive."

"Why are you meetin' here?"

7

"Because he asked me to."

"And he didn't say why?"

"No," Clint said, "he didn't have to."

"He must be a really good friend."

"He is."

She studied him for a moment, then said, "You look like a man who knows how to use his gun."

"When I have to."

"You and your friend aren't planning anythin' bad, are you? Like a robbery?"

"Not likely," Clint said. "That's not something we do."

She visibly relaxed and said, "Good."

"Why are you asking?"

"I don't like the men, here," she said, "so when a stranger comes to town, I'm interested."

"What's wrong with the men here?" he asked.

"They're only interested in two things," she said, "bourbon and horse racing."

"And you don't like either?"

"No." She stood up. "I like men who are interested in somethin' else."

Before he could ask her what she meant, another table with three men seated at it called her over.

"Don't leave," she said, "without talkin' to me again."

"I won't," he promised.

Chapter Three

At a quarter-to-midnight Bat still had not arrived. Clint pushed his last half-warm beer away preparing to leave.

"Are you leavin'?" Lisa asked, running over.

"I was planning to."

"I'm going to leave, too. Would you walk me home?"

"Are you expecting trouble?"

"A couple of fellas didn't like it when I rejected them earlier tonight," she explained. "I think they might be waiting for me outside."

"All right," he said, "I'd be happy to."

"Let me just get my wrap," she told him and ran upstairs.

The bartender came over and collected Clint's last glass.

"Lisa's a good kid," he said. "Go easy with her."

"I will," Clint said, "although I'm surprised she'd want somebody to walk her home."

"Walk her home?" the bartender said, looking puzzled. "But she has a room upstairs.

"But she—" Clint started, then stopped. "Oh, I think I get it."

"Just be nice to her," the barman said, and went back to work.

Clint felt pretty sure he knew what the pretty girl had in mind, and he wasn't against it. But he thought he would allow the girl to continue calling the shots and see where everything went. After all, he didn't have a better way to spend the night.

He sat back down to wait for Lisa, but he had barely done so when she came back down, a brown shawl covering her shoulders.

"Shall we go?" she asked.

"By all means."

They walked out of the almost empty saloon and started off down the street.

"Where are we going?" he asked her.

"Your hotel," she said.

"I thought I was walking you home," he said,

"Actually," she said, "I wasn't exactly truthful about that. You see, I live in a room upstairs from the saloon."

"I know that."

"Did Barney open his big mouth?"

"Barney?"

"The bartender."

"Well, yes," Clint said, "he did manage to mention that."

"What else did he have to say?"

"Just that he wanted me to be nice to you."

"That's good advice," she said.

"Why don't you get together with Barney?" Clint asked her.

"For the same reason I don't get together with anyone else in town. Bourbon and beer."

"Barney doesn't have a choice, does he?" Clint asked. "He *is* a bartender."

"I know, but he takes it too seriously," she said. "Your hotel is on the next street."

"So, *you're* walking *me* home, eh?"

"That's about the size of it," she said.

"Let me get this straight," he said. "We're going to spend the night together."

"That's right."

"Because you don't like any of the local men."

"And because I won't have to deal with you living here, afterward."

"I see."

She stopped walking and asked, "There is no chance you'll live here, is there?"

"None whatsoever."

She grabbed his arm and said, "Then let's go up-stairs."

***

When they got to Clint's room, Lisa very calmly be-gan to remove all her clothes. Clint stood transfixed in the center of the room as the lovely young woman disrobed. She had small, teacup breasts with dark nipples and very smooth skin.

"Is somethin' wrong?" she asked.

"No, nothing," Clint said. "You're very beautiful."

"Thank you."

"And very young," he added. "Are you sure you want to do this?"

"Oh, very much so," she said. "I may be young, but I'm no virgin. I know what I want and, more importantly, I know what I don't want."

She approached him and reached for his gunbelt.

"Don't touch my gun!" he snapped.

She pulled her hands back as if she had been burned.

"I'm sorry," she said. "I didn't realize . . . you're a gunfighter?"

"Not really," he said. "But I do depend heavily on my gun for my life."

She took a few steps back.

"I suppose I should've asked you for your name," she said. "Are you wanted by the law?"

"No, nothing like that," he said, unbuckling his gun-belt. He walked to the bedpost and hung it there, then turned to face her.

"My name is Clint Adams."

Her eyes widened.

"You-you're the Gunsmith?"

"That's right," he said, sitting on the bed to remove his boots. "If that changes your mind about being here, I'll understand."

He studied the naked girl, listened for footsteps outside in the hall. Maybe she was supposed to distract him so someone could sneak up on him. That had never happened, no matter how beautiful the girl with him had been. But he was always aware of his surroundings, and at the moment he heard nothing outside the room.

"Mr. Adams?" she said walking over to him. "Clint. I'm not changing my mind."

He removed his second boot and looked at her.

"I wanted to spend the night with you before I knew who you were," she said, placing her head on his shoulder. "Now that I do, it hasn't changed my mind."

She sat next to him and pressed her hot flesh against him. At the same time, she used one hand to undo the buttons of his shirt and slid it inside to rub his chest. Then she took her hand out and turned his face so she could kiss him.

Chapter Four

Lisa proved what she said about not being a virgin was true.

When Clint tossed his second boot aside, Lisa straddled him, kissed him on the mouth, then the neck, and moved on to his chest. She peeled his shirt off and threw it across the room, then got on her knees and undid his belt. With his help she pulled his trousers off, and left him naked, with his hard cock poking up at her.

"Oh, my," she said fondling him with both hands.

Leaning forward she took him into her mouth. She bobbed her head up and down, sucking him avidly, until she could feel he was ready to finish, then quickly released him and leaped into his lap so that he pierced her deeply and fully. She gasped and froze for a moment, then started to move up and down on his lap.

Clint allowed her to bounce on him until he wasn't sure he could take it anymore. At that point he knew he had to take command, or it would all be over too soon. He grabbed her by the hips, lifted her off him, stood and deposited her onto the bed, on her back. He then spread her legs wide, holding her by the ankles, and drove himself into her again.

"Oh, yes!" Lisa growled. "I knew it."

Clint was too busy to wonder what it was she knew. He continued to pound into her until her words became grunts. He released her ankles and climbed onto the bed between her widespread legs to continue driving himself into her with increasing speed. Eventually, the bed itself began to take little hops across the room until it had worked its way away from the wall. At one point it seemed as if the bed rail might come loose, dumping Clint's gun to the floor. But eventually they found a rhythm that kept the bed in place rather than moving it across the floor. When their pleasure peaked, they pressed together as if they were trying to climb inside each other . . .

***

"You knew what?" he asked, later.

"What?" she gasped, still trying to catch her breath.

"At one point you said 'I knew it,' " he told her. "Knew what?"

"Oh," she said, brushing her hair out of her face, where strands of it were plastered to her by her perspiration, "I knew you'd be different from any other man I've ever been with."

"And that's a good thing, right?"

"Oh, yes," she said, "a very good thing. Like I told you, the men in this town only care about two things."

"Bourbon . . ."

"And . . . and horses."

"All horses?"

"The horses that run at Churchill Downs."

"Like in the Derby?"

"Yes," she said. "You know about the Derby?"

"I was here once, a while back," Clint said.

"Why?"

"I wanted to see the Derby."

"So why are you back?" she asked. "The Kentucky Derby was last month."

"I told you," he said. "I'm here to see a friend."

"But you don't know why."

"No."

"And you trust this friend enough to just come, when he calls?"

"We trust each other," Clint said. "When one of us needs help, the other comes."

"How many friends do you have like that?" she asked, propping herself up on an elbow. Her long hair fell down and covered her naked breasts.

"I can count them on one hand," he answered.

"Well," she said, cuddling up to him, "right now I have something else for you to do with that hand."

16

Chapter Five

Lisa stayed the entire night with Clint, so they were able to make love several more times before they fell asleep. In the morning she rose first, and he watched with pleasure as she dressed.

"I have to get back to my room, clean up and put on some fresh clothes. Then I have some shopping to do. What will you be doing?"

"I'm going to see if my friend shows up at the Shamrock."

"The saloon doesn't open til noon," she told him. "What will you do til then?"

"First I'll get some more rest. You wore me out pretty good, last night. Then I'll get some breakfast downstairs. After that I'll take a look around town to see how much Louisville has changed since I was here last."

"Guess I'll see you at the Shamrock later," she said.

She walked to the bed and kissed him, then said, "I hope you don't put too much meaning into this, Clint. I'm really not a one-man woman—although I may not have found a man I wanted to belong to, until now.

"Lisa," Clint said, but she cut him off with a laugh.

"Don't panic," she said. "I'm kidding. I know you won't be staying in Louisville. We'll just have some fun before you leave, if we have time."

She left the room, and Clint dozed off.

***

Lisa was right about the hotel dining room. It served a tasty array of breakfasts. One of them was French Toast.

French Toast originated in the Roman Empire and, over the years, had appeared the world over in different recipes. It was served in sweet and savory fashion. Clint's hotel, the Bluegrass, served it sweet with sugar, fruit and syrup.

"You can have it with strawberries or blueberries," the waiter told Clint.

"I'll take strawberries."

"And we can accompany it with bacon."

"Sounds great!"

"How would you like your coffee?" the middle-aged waiter asked.

"Strong and black," Clint said.

"Good man!" the waiter said. "I'll be right back with it."

The waiter returned with a small pot of coffee. He filled Clint's cup and left the pot on the table.

Clint was on his second cup when the waiter returned with a plate of French Toast and bacon, covered with strawberries, powdered sugar and syrup.

"Enjoy," the man told him.

"I intend to," Clint said, and dug in. After his first bite, he ate with gusto and accepted the waiter's offer of a second helping.

He was finishing his second plate when the desk clerk came into the dining room. It was the same young man who had checked him in when he arrived. Bat had not only asked Clint in a telegram to meet him in Louisville at The Shamrock Saloon, but had told Clint to stay in the Bluegrass Hotel, where a room would be waiting for him.

"Mr. Adams," the clerk said, "A telegram came for you."

"A telegram? From Bat Masterson?" It was a stupid question. Bat was the only one who knew he was in Louisville.

"I don't know, sir," the clerk said. "The telegraph operator delivered it, and I didn't read it." He handed it to Clint, who chose to believe him.

"Okay, thanks."

He tipped the clerk, who returned to the lobby.

When Clint unfolded the telegram, he saw that it was, indeed, from Bat.

BEEN DELAYED. CAUGHT A BULLET. NOT BAD, BUT WILL BE A WEEK. FIND MAD MCCALL. THE OWNER OF THE SHAMROCK WILL TELL YOU WHERE. HE WILL EXPLAIN.

There were any number of reasons Bat might have caught a bullet. A sore loser in a poker game, or somebody wanting to make a name for himself. Even when you expected a bullet as Clint and Bat Masterson did, you couldn't always avoid it. So Bat had been shot, but if he expected to only be delayed a week, it probably wasn't a serious wound.

Clint refolded the telegram and stuck it in his shirt pocket, then finished his second plate, and another pot of coffee before paying his bill.

"It was good, huh?" the waiter asked.

"It must've been. I had two plates."

"Gonna be in town a while?"

"Looks like it," Clint said.

"Good, you can try some of our other breakfasts."

"What about supper?"

The waiter made a face.

"That's a different cook," he said. "You're better off eatin' somewhere else. There are a few good cafes around."

"Thanks for the warning."

Clint tipped the waiter and left the hotel.

Chapter Six

Clint stopped just outside the hotel door and sat in a chair on the porch. He now knew he was going to have to wait at least a week for Bat Masterson. That didn't really change his plans for the day. He could still walk around town til noon, and then go to the Shamrock to talk to the owner about finding somebody named Mad McCall.

He was in the act of standing when five women suddenly came out the front door. They were all wearing long gingham dresses of different colors and carrying handwritten placards. They were arguing amongst themselves about something. Two of them jostled him, causing him to fall back into his chair.

"Oh, excuse us," one of the women said, turning to look at him. "We're sorry."

"That's all right, Ma'am," Clint said. "No harm done."

"We're with the WCTU, and I'm afraid we were arguing and not lookin' where we were goin'," the woman went on.

"*You* weren't lookin' where you were goin', Milly," another woman said. "Too busy trying to give orders."

"That's because I'm in charge, Gretchen."

The two women glared at each other. Milly was older, in her fifties, and stockily built, hence she was able to knock Clint over. Gretchen looked to be in her thirties. While Milly had a face that would scare children, Gretchen had the face of an angel.

"WCTU?" he asked.

"We are with the Woman's Christian Temperance League," Gretchen said to him. "Do you partake of liquor, sir?"

"I have a beer on occasion," Clint admitted.

"That's as bad as whiskey," one of the other women said. "You should attend one of our meetings, and we'll tell you of the wickedness of drinkin'."

"Well, maybe I'll do that, Ma'am."

"Come along, ladies," Milly said. "We have a lot of work to do."

"Again," Gretchen said to Clint, "we're so very, very sorry."

"Don't apologize to him, Gretchen," another woman said. "He's obviously a sinner."

As the women walked across the street, Clint heard Gretchen say, "You can't judge people so harshly, Harriet." She looked back and gave Clint a wan smile. He touched the brim of his hat.

The women continued to bicker as they reached the other side of the street.

Chapter Seven

Clint had a look at the growth of Louisville until quarter til noon, then started for the Shamrock. He was standing out front when the doors opened at twelve-oh-five.

"Anxious for a drink?" the bartender asked, with a smile.

"I'd go for a coffee," Clint said.

"You got it," the barman said. "Come on in."

Clint followed the man to the bar, where the man poured him a cup of coffee.

"What brings you around so early?" the man asked him. "Lisa?"

"No," Clint said, "I want to meet the owner."

"Is there a problem?"

"No," Clint said, "a friend of mine told me to look him up."

"Well," the bartender said," he's got an office upstairs, but he should be down shortly for a late breakfast. You could wait for him."

"That'll be fine," Clint said. "What's his name?"

"Henry Boudreau."

"Is he French?"

"French name, but he's all American."

"Do you know a man named Mad McCall?"

"Never heard of him," the bartender said, but Clint wasn't sure he was telling the truth.

"Okay, thanks for the coffee. I'll drink it over here."

He reached into his pocket for money, but the barman said, "Forget it."

"Thanks."

Clint carried the cup to a table against the wall and sat. Men started to drift in and stand at the bar, since there were no games going yet. Eventually, a well-dressed man appeared at the top of the steps and came down. He exchanged nods with the bartender, then went through a curtain into a back room. Clint got up and walked to the bar.

"Okay to go back and talk to the boss?" he asked.

"If you take him his breakfast."

"Suits me."

"I'll be a minute."

The bartender went into the kitchen behind the bar, came out carrying a plate of bacon-and-eggs and a cup of coffee.

"Here you go," he said.

Clint accepted the breakfast and walked into the back room. The man was seated at a round, green felt covered table, fiddling with a deck of cards.

"Okay if I come in?" Clint asked.

"If that's for me, it is," Boudreau said.

"It is." Clint stepped forward and set the food down. Boudreau laid his cards aside and picked up his fork.

"Are we hirin' waiters now?"

"No," Clint said, "I told the bartender I wanted to meet you."

"That right? Who are you?"

"My name's Clint Adams."

Boudreau was surprised.

"What the hell are you doin' here?" he asked.

"Mind if I sit?"

"Sure, go ahead."

Clint sat across from him.

"Want some breakfast?" the saloon owner asked.

"I had my breakfast," Clint said, "and the bartender gave me some coffee."

"Well then, you might as well tell me what's on your mind," Boudreau said.

"Bat Masterson," Clint said. "He suggested I come and see you."

"That's right, you and Bat are good friends," Boudreau said. "What did he have in mind, puttin' us together?"

"He asked me to meet him here in Louisville, at this saloon. I got a telegram from him this morning that he'll be late." He didn't bother telling Boudreau that Bat had been shot.

"He also told me I should find a fella named Mad McCall. Said you could tell me where to look."

"McCall?" Boudreau stopped chewing. "Why's he want you to find McCall?"

"I was hoping you could tell me," Clint said. "Or McCall would, when I found him. What's he do, anyway?"

"McCall's a gunhand," Boudreau said.

"Any good?"

"Never been outdrawn or out-shot."

"Not even by Bat?"

"They've never gone up against each other," Boudreau said, going back to his breakfast. "You think that's what Bat wants you for?"

"Bat's got his own gun, he never puts out a call for mine."

"Then why are you here?"

"I don't know," Clint said. "That's what I'm going to find out, either when you tell me where McCall is, or when Bat gets here."

"I can't tell you where he is, but I can find 'im and put you two together."

"I'd be obliged if you'd do it," Clint said.

"Where are you stayin'?"

"The Bluegrass."

"That figures," Boudreau said. "Best hotel in town."

"Well," Clint said, standing, "that's where I'll be when you locate McCall. Either there, or in here."

"Glad to have your business," Boudreau said.

"Enjoy your breakfast," Clint said, and left.

***

Clint stopped at the bar and left his empty cup there.

"Everythin' okay?" the bartender asked.

"So far," Clint said. "Your boss seemed happy with his breakfast."

"You gonna wait around for Lisa?"

"No, I'll see her later in here."

"See ya then."

Clint walked to the front door, but as he left he was jostled by a rather solid body in a dress.

"Well," he said to the women of the WCTU, "we meet again."

"Why am I not surprised to see you leaving a saloon this early in the day?" Milly asked.

"Milly," Gretchen said, "leave the man be."

"You're too soft for this job, Gretchen," Milly said, and marched inside, followed by the other women.

"I'm sorry," Gretchen said, and followed them.

"Where is the proprietor?" Clint heard Milly demand.

Chapter Eight

The telegram from Bat Masterson had come from Denver. That was also where the first one had come from. Clint decided to go to the telegraph office and send one back. He wanted a little more information.

He wrote the telegram out for the clerk and passed it to him.

"Bat Masterson in Denver, yes, sir," the young man said. "You gonna wait for a reply?"

"No," Clint said. "Drop it off at the Bluegrass, will you?" He paid the man a little extra.

"Yes, sir, I'll do that," the man said.

"Thanks."

Clint left the office, stopped just outside to decide his next move. If the horses were running at the track he would have gone there for the afternoon. Poker was a possibility, but there were probably no games going on this early. And he didn't want to go back to the Shamrock just yet. He didn't want to run into the temperance women, again. He decided to walk around a part of town he hadn't seen yet, maybe stop somewhere else for a drink. It was a pleasant enough way to spend an afternoon.

***

He stopped in a small saloon called The Bandana, stood at the bar and ordered a beer. There were a few other men there, having an afternoon drink. The place wasn't big enough to have girls working the floor, or to have table games going on. It was a good place to just stand and nurse an afternoon drink, which was what Clint did.

***

After Boudreau fended off the women of the temperance league, he went to the bar to talk to his bartender.

"Barney," he said, "who knows where Mad McCall is?"

"Probably Chase Bennett, boss."

"And where's Bennett?"

"We wait long enough he'll be in here."

"Okay," Boudreau said, "when he arrives, tell him I want McCall."

"I'll tell 'im, boss," Barney said. "What's this about?"

"The Gunsmith wants him."

"The Gunsmith and McCall?" Boudreau said, "That'll be somethin' to see."

"I don't think he wants him for that."

"Then what fer?"

"We'll all find that out, soon enough," Boudreau said. "I'll be upstairs doin' some paperwork for a while. Be down later."

"Right."

Boudreau went upstairs and locked himself in his room, which was also his office.

***

Clint listened to snippets of conversation around him. He realized Lisa was right. All he heard the men talking about was bourbon and horses. When he got tired of listening, he finished his beer and left The Bandana.

He walked back to his hotel and stopped at the desk to see if he had a telegram.

"Yes, sir," the clerk said, "came in about an hour ago."

The clerk handed it to Clint.

"Thanks."

He could have read it in the lobby, but he decided to take it to his room. He unfolded it and read the words on it.

BE PATIENT. GOT SOME BUSINESS.

I'LL BE THERE SOON.

He wasn't used to Bat playing these kinds of games, but apparently he was going to have to wait.

Chapter Nine

There were a lot of ears in and out of the Shamrock during the course of one day, and on this one the word went out about the Gunsmith being in town.

Andy Calhoun heard the news, and immediately brought it to Griff Kendall at his brewery, which was a new business for the man.

"Wait," Griff said, "say that again?"

Clint Adams is in town," Calhoun said. "He was seen at the Shamrock."

"What's he doin' here?" Griff asked. "How long is he here for?"

"I don't know," Calhoun said. "I only know that he's here."

"Do you know what hotel he's stayin' at?" Griff asked.

"No," Calhoun said, "but I guess I could find out."

"Then do it, Andy," Griff said. "Do you know what this means? Instead of brewing Kendall Beer," Griff said, "I can brew Gunsmith beer."

"Wouldn't you need his permission for that?" Calhoun asked.

"Yes, I would," Griff said, "and with him bein' here in Louisville, I can get it."

"You think he'd go for it?"

"Would he go for gettin' rich and famous?" Griff asked. "Who wouldn't?"

"But he's already famous."

"I'm gonna put it to him so he can't refuse," Griff said. "Jesus, I've been tryin' to come up with a plan to launch my brew, and now this is it."

"But what if—"

"There's no what if," Griff said. "You just get out there and find 'im for me!"

Calhoun hesitated.

"What's in it for me?" he asked.

"If I get him to front my brew," Griff said, "you get a percentage."

"How big?"

"We can talk about that when the time comes," Griff said. "First let's get the Gunsmith."

That made sense to Calhoun, who turned and left the building.

***

Griffin Kendall had been trying to launch a new brewery for close to a year, but without luck. He had already tried several different names, but now he thought he had something. All he needed was the Gunsmith's cooperation, and he would not only be able to launch his beer, but maybe even his own brand of bourbon.

All he needed was the Gunsmith.

***

That evening Clint went back to the Shamrock, hoping Boudreau had located Mad McCall for him. The place was crowded, but he got a spot at the bar and waved Barney over.

"Hello, Mr. Adams," the bartender said, "Beer?"

"Yes, please."

When Barney set a cold one down in front of him, Clint asked, "Do you know if your boss found McCall?"

"He's got feelers out, Mr. Adams," the barman said. "Should be soon."

"Yeah, okay, thanks."

Clint picked up his beer and turned, leaned back against the bar. He saw Lisa working the floor, along with two other girls, bringing beer and whiskey to the men seated at tables, some of which had games going. He saw Faro, Poker and Blackjack, but he wasn't in the mood for any of them. He figured to finish his beer and then go to his hotel.

After he drained his glass he set it down, and saw Lisa coming toward him.

"Hi, Clint."

"Hello, Lisa."

"I'm workin' til late tonight, but I might be able to come over later on," she told him.

"That's okay," Clint said. "I'll be around for at least a week."

"Well, I have a couple of days off next week," Lisa said. "Maybe then?"

"Yeah, sure," he said. "Maybe then."

"Good, Clint. I've got a table waitin'."

She went to get her drinks from the bar, as Clint went out the door.

***

As he crossed the lobby of his hotel to the stairs the desk clerk waved to him.

"What can I do for you?" Clint asked.

"I thought you'd like to know," the clerk said. "Somebody was in here askin' about you."

"What'd they want to know?"

"If you were stayin' here," the clerk said. "I think he was askin' around town at other hotels, too."

"Did you know him?"

"No, sir, I never saw him before."

"What'd he look like?"

"I dunno," the clerk said. "Thirties, average height, brown hair."

Clint didn't know what Mad McCall looked like, but didn't know who else would be looking for him.

"What'd you tell him?"

"Nothin'."

"Good. Thanks for letting me know."

"Yes, sir."

Clint tipped the young man and went to his room.

Chapter Ten

Mad McCall came into the Shamrock about an hour later. A big man, he didn't need to make room at the bar for himself. Men just naturally moved out of his way.

"Hey, Barney," he greeted.

"McCall," Barney said. "Whiskey?"

"Beer, this time," McCall said. "I heard Boudreau's lookin' for me."

"He is," Barney said, setting a beer down. "I'll tell 'im you're here."

"Fine."

Barney came out from behind the bar and went up to his boss' office.

"McCall's here," he said, when the man opened his door.

"Put him in the back room," Boudreau said, "I'll be right down."

"Sure, boss."

"And give 'im his drinks."

"Right."

Barney went back down and set Mad McCall up in the back room with a couple of beers. When Boudreau walked in, he was into the second one.

"Thanks for comin', Mad," Boudreau said, sitting across from him.

"What's on your mind, Boudreau?"

"Not me," Boudreau said. "Clint Adams was in here lookin' for you."

"For me? What's the Gunsmith want with me?"

"Well, first he said he was looking for Bat Masterson. Then he said Masterson was going to be late, but told Adams to look you up."

"Did he say why?"

"No, he just asked if I could find you."

McCall rubbed his jaw, finished his beer.

"He say where he was stayin'?" McCall asked.

"The Bluegrass."

"Okay." McCall stood up.

"Where are you goin'?" Boudreau asked.

"Where else? The Bluegrass. Thanks."

"Let me know what's goin' on, okay?"

"Sure," McCall said. "Depending on what it turns out to be. Thanks for the beers."

McCall left. Boudreau sat back, wondering what was going on.

***

When Clint got to his room he removed his boots and sat in a chair. He figured whoever was looking for him, probably wasn't Mad McCall. Boudreau would have told McCall what hotel Clint was in. So somebody else heard he was in town, and was looking for him. Clint decided rather than going looking for McCall, he would wait for the man to find him.

***

Down in the lobby Mad McCall approached the front desk.

"What can I do for you, sir?" the clerk asked, looking up at the big man.

"I'm looking for Clint Adams. What room is he in?"

"Who?"

"Don't play dumb," McCall said. "I was told he's lookin' for me, and he's stayin' here."

"Well . . . there was another man here lookin' for him," the clerk said. "I'm not supposed to talk about our guests."

"Then don't," McCall said. "Just turn your back for a minute."

"Huh?"

McCall made a motion with his hand for the clerk to turn around.

"Oh, uh, okay . . ."

The clerk turned his back and McCall grabbed the registration book to take a look. He found Clint's name and room number.

"Okay," he said to the clerk. "Thanks."

The clerk turned around and asked, "Am I gonna get in trouble?"

"No trouble at all," McCall said, and walked to the stairs.

***

Clint heard heavy footsteps coming down the hall from the stairs. They certainly didn't sound like Lisa. He stood up and waited, his hand down by his gun.

The knock on the door was hard.

"Who is it?" Clint asked.

"McCall. I heard you was lookin' for me."

"How do I know you're McCall?" Clint asked.

"Henry Boudreau told me you was lookin' for me and told me where to find you."

"Okay," Clint said, "are you armed?"

"Yeah, I'm wearin' a gun."

"Keep your hands at your sides while I open the door."

"Look," McCall said, "I know you're the Gunsmith. I'm gonna keep my hand away from my gun, don't you worry."

Clint opened the door.

Chapter Eleven

A very large man stood in the hallway, his hands held out at his sides, away from the gun on his right hip.

"Mad McCall?" Clint asked.

"That's right," the man said, "and you're Clint Adams."

"Right."

"We gonna do this here, in the hall?" McCall asked.

"Come on in," Clint said, stepping back.

McCall stepped into the room, which immediately felt smaller.

"I don't have anything to offer you," Clint said, closing the door.

"That's okay, I just had two beers at the Shamrock," McCall said, then added, "free."

"Have a seat, then."

McCall sat in the single armchair, while Clint sat on the bed, his gun still in his holster.

"You want my gun?" McCall asked.

"No, keep it," Clint said. "Now, what's this about?"

"I thought I was here for you to tell me that," McCall said.

"I'm in Louisville to meet up with Bat Masterson," Clint said, "but he's been delayed by a bullet."

"What? How bad?"

"His telegram from Denver said not too bad, but he also suggested I find you. Have you heard from him?"

"Not for a couple of months," McCall said, "but he said somebody else might be lookin' for me. He just never said anythin' about you."

"I guess he wasn't sure whose help he was going to ask for," Clint said. "Do you know what this is about?"

"I might," McCall said, "if it's the same thing me and him talked about a couple of months ago, when he was here."

"And what was that?"

"Whiskey."

"That seems to be something folks hereabouts are real interested in," Clint said. "Whiskey and horses."

"Actually," McCall said, "it's whiskey, beer and horses."

"Bourbon, specifically?" Clint asked.

"Yep," McCall said. "Drinking it and making it."

"So what is Bat getting involved in?" Clint asked.

"Makin' it."

"Why?" Clint asked. "I've never known Bat to be interested in producing whiskey before."

"He never was," McCall said, "until he won a distillery in a poker game."

"Now that figures," Clint said.

"It was a pretty high stakes game, and Bat had just about wiped everyone out, except a fella named Teller."

"And Teller put up the distillery to cover his bet?"

"Half interest," McCall said. "He had Kings full in his hand."

"And Bat?"

"Filled a straight flush," McCall said, "two thru six of spades."

"Jesus. Did Teller try to put up the other half?"

"He was considering it, but Bat wouldn't let him. He preferred a partnership with somebody who knew what he was doing, to owning the entire thing when he knew nothing about it at all. So they became partners."

"Teller/Masterson?" Clint asked.

"No, Bat kept his name off it. He's a silent partner."

"So what's he want from me?" Clint asked. "I'm not interested in owning shares in a distillery."

"I don't know what Bat wants from you," McCall said. "He just told me that somebody might come to town looking for him, and if he wasn't here they'd find me."

"How long have you known Bat?" Clint asked.

"More than ten years. You?"

"We go back to the buffalo hunting days," Clint said.

"I only met him because he came here from time to time for poker and horse racing. He also refereed a fight here."

"Yeah," Clint said, "he's more of a sportsman these days, although he's also dabbling in becoming a newspaperman."

"Bat can pretty much do anythin' he wants," McCall said.

"Do you play poker?" Clint asked.

"No," McCall said, "Bat and I would drink together, and there were times when he needed somebody to watch his back."

"And he trusted you to do that?" Clint asked.

"The times that I did it," McCall said, "there was nobody else around. I'm sure if you was here, it woulda been different."

Clint got quiet.

"Whataya thinkin'?" McCall asked.

"I'm wondering if Bat getting shot has anything to do with this distillery," Clint said, "and maybe he asked me to come here to help him. But since he's going to be late, maybe he's putting us together so you can catch my back."

"But you say he got shot in Denver," McCall said. "That's pretty far away. There are a lot of reasons men like us and Bat can get shot."

"That's true."

"I guess we'll have to wait til he gets here to find out for sure what happened."

"I agree."

"If you want me to watch your back til he gets here, I'm happy to," McCall said.

"It doesn't sound like a bad idea," Clint said.

"Meantime," McCall said, "maybe you'd like to meet Ben Teller and take a look at his distillery."

"How much do you know about Teller?" Clint asked.

"He's been a fixture here in Louisville for a lot of years," McCall said.

"How old is he?"

"About sixty."

"Do you think he might have sent somebody to kill Bat so he wouldn't have to share his business?"

"Everythin' I know about Teller," McCall said, "that doesn't seem likely. In fact, he was pretty happy to have somebody like Bat Masterson as a partner."

"Then I guess we'll just have to wait until Bat recovers enough to show up here in Louisville."

Clint stood up and McCall followed. The two men shook hands and agreed to meet in the lobby in the morning.

Chapter Twelve

When Andy Calhoun told Griff Kendall he hadn't located Clint Adams, the man didn't accept it.

"You can't tell me the Gunsmith is in Louisville, but nobody knows where he is. That can't be possible."

"I swear, I checked all of the likely hotels in town," Calhoun claimed.

"You checked every register?"

"Well, no . . ."

"What'd you do?"

"I asked at the desk."

"And don't you think a man like Clint Adams would leave instructions for them not to give away the fact that he was there?"

"Well . . ."

"Come on, Andy," Kendall said, "if you want a share, you've gotta earn it. Get back out there and find that man for me!"

"Yeah, yeah, okay, Griff. I will."

Calhoun practically ran out the door. He would start his search anew come morning . . .

***

Clint did some thinking that night. If he was there because of Bat's half interest in a bourbon distillery, it didn't make any sense to him. Bat Masterson had many business interests of his own, without including any of his friends. Why would he choose to involve Clint in this one?

It frustrated Clint that he would have to wait for Bat to arrive to find out.

***

Over breakfast in the hotel dining room, Clint and McCall discussed what they should do while waiting for their friend to arrive in Louisville.

"I can get you a poker game," McCall offered.

"I could get one at the Shamrock," Clint said. "I'm not really interested."

"Then what does interest you?" McCall asked.

"How about giving me a look at this distillery Bat owns half of?" Clint asked.

"Hey, if that's what ya want, I can show it to you from the outside," McCall said. "If ya want a look at the inside, you'll hafta meet Ben Teller."

"Let's hold off on that for now," Clint said. "I don't want it getting around yet that I'm in town. Somebody's already been looking for me in the hotel."

"The clerk told me that," McCall said. "If some-body's goin' from hotel to hotel, tryin' to find out where you are, I can find out who it is."

"That's a good idea, too," Clint said. "Do you have to do that yourself, or can you put out the word?"

"I can put out the word so nobody knows we're lookin'," McCall said.

"Good," Clint said, "let's do that then."

McCall looked across the table at Clint, over his fork-ful of something the chef called a Spanish Omelet.

"Can we finish here, first. This is the best damned breakfast I ever had."

"You live in town and you've never eaten here?"

"This place is a little too high-toned for me. You saw the way the waiter looked at me."

"I'm not any more high-toned than you are," Clint told him.

"Yeah, but Bat probably arranged this place for you," McCall reminded him.

"You're right about that," Clint said. "Bat's a little more posh than both of us. Sure, you go ahead and finish eating. We're in no rush."

They both went back to their breakfasts.

Chapter Thirteen

After breakfast Clint and McCall went out front.

"You got a horse?" McCall asked.

"Yes," Clint said, "he's in the hotel stable. What about you?"

"Sometimes I have one," McCall said, "but these days I don't. I can rent one in the stable, though. Come on, the distillery's too far to walk."

They circled around to the back of the hotel where the livery was. While Clint saddled his Tobiano, McCall arranged for a mount. Clint was waiting outside when the big man walked out with an eight-year-old dun.

"He looks solid," Clint said. "How much did he go for?"

"Turns out I know the hostler," McCall said. "He loaned me this one."

They mounted up and McCall took the lead.

***

The distillery was on the other side of town, in a neighborhood of two-story brick warehouses, breweries and distilleries. The one they stopped across the street from had no name on the outside.

"That's it," McCall said.

"No name?"

"Not yet," McCall said. "Teller was gonna call it the Teller Brewery when he was brewing beer. When he branched out to bourbon, he was gonna call it the Teller Distillery. Then when Bat won half of it he said he didn't want his name on it, at all. I guess they haven't come up with one yet."

"It looks like a solid investment, from the outside," Clint commented.

"You want to take a look inside?"

"No, I don't want to meet Teller, yet."

"You don't hafta meet him," McCall said. "And even if you do, he don't hafta know who you are. We can go in, meet one of his workers and have a little taste."

Clint gave the suggestion a thought and decided to go ahead.

"Let's do it," he agreed. "I might as well taste what Bat's got his money invested in."

They dismounted across the street and tied their horses off, then crossed over to the front door.

"They keep it locked?" Clint asked.

"Nobody does, not during the day. They want folks comin' in and sampling the product."

McCall opened the door and they entered. They were in a small area with a young man behind the counter.

"Hey, Gents," the man said, "what can I do for you?"

"We thought we'd sample what you got," McCall said. "We might be interested in a big purchase."

"Sure thing," the young man said, "bourbon or beer?"

"We'll taste both," Clint said. "Is the boss around?"

"Not today," the man said, "but I can give you a sample. Come on."

He came from around the counter and Clint and McCall followed him through a door.

***

The young man's name was Danny. He showed Clint and McCall the operation, and then gave them each a taste of several vats and barrels.

"Well, whataya think, Gents?" Danny asked.

"Not bad," Clint said.

"How much are you interested in?"

"We'll have to talk it over and get back to you," McCall said.

"Well, you should know that a famous name's gonna be buyin' into the place. If you're gonna buy you better make it soon, before the price goes up."

"Thanks for the warning," Clint said. "We'll get back to you."

Chapter Fourteen

Clint and McCall crossed the street to their horses and paused there.

"He sounds pretty sure Bat's gonna come out from behind," McCall said.

"If it's Bat," Clint said.

"Whataya mean?"

"What if Teller's got somebody else lined up?" Clint asked.

"Why would he, with Bat as half owner?" McCall asked.

"Is Teller on the level?" Clint asked.

"I told you, he's been at this a long time," McCall told him.

"Maybe he's tired of trying so hard," Clint said. "With Bat involved, he may not have to. On the other hand, the more the merrier. Maybe Teller has sold more halves."

"You're thinkin' Teller's crooked?"

"Guess I'm just suspicious, but who knows?"

"Are you thinkin' Teller lost half his place on purpose?" McCall asked.

"No, Bat's not that gullible," Clint said. "Like I said, maybe I'm just too suspicious."

"Let's get a drink, somewhere," McCall suggested.

"You didn't get enough inside?" Clint teased.

***

McCall took Clint to a saloon nearby. It was early afternoon, and the place wasn't busy. There was only a lone bartender at work. They went to the bar and ordered a beer.

"What now?" McCall asked.

"Bat's not going to be here for at least a week," Clint said. "I can't think of what I can do until then."

"You play poker, don't you?"

"I've been known to."

"Well, like I said, I can arrange a game."

"Did you arrange the game during which Bat won half Teller's distillery?"

"Naw, that wasn't me," McCall said. "As a matter of fact, I only heard about it after. Wait a minute," McCall stood up straight, angrily, "were you thinkin' I set Bat up?"

Clint was suddenly very wary of how much bigger and stronger McCall was than him.

"No, no," Clint said, waving a hand, "hang on, I'm not saying that."

The fire in McCall's eyes cooled off.

"Tell me something," Clint said, "why do they call you Mad McCall?"

McCall turned back to the bar and grabbed his beer.

"Some folks seem to think I got a quick temper."

"Remind me not to get you mad," Clint said, leaning over his own beer.

***

Griff Kendall looked up from his desk when the office door opened and Andy Calhoun came in.

"I found 'im!"

"Adams?"

"Well," Calhoun said, "I found his hotel."

"Siddown and have a drink, Andy," Kendall said. He reached behind him and grabbed a bottle. "My best stuff."

He poured a glass and pushed it across the desk to Calhoun, who grabbed it and drank it down.

"Okay," Kendall said, "where is he?"

"He's got a room at the Bluegrass Hotel."

Kendall raised his eyebrows.

"That's a nice place," he said. "Adams must have money."

"I dunno," Calhoun said. "His reputation's for guns, not money, ain't it?"

"As far as I know," Kendall said.

"So whataya gonna do now?"

"Well, later today I may go over to the hotel and pay Mr. Adams a visit and discuss some business with 'im."

"You think he'll go for the idea?"

"I don't know, yet," Kendall said. "I haven't decided just what my idea's gonna be."

"You want him to back you, don't ya?"

"I don't know," Kendall said. "I still have some thinkin' to do. You better get goin'."

"Where? To do what?"

"I don't care, Andy," Kendall said. "Just go. I'm done with you . . . for now."

***

After Calhoun left, Kendall got out a clean glass and poured himself some of his best bourbon. He sat back in his chair and sipped while he considered what his approach to the Gunsmith should be. Andy had a good idea about getting Adams to back his brand, but something else occurred to Kendall while Calhoun was talking, which was why he wanted Andy out of the picture while he mulled it over.

His brand would probably soar if he could get Clint Adams' Gunsmith moniker right on the bottles!

Chapter Fifteen

Mad McCall offered to give Clint a tour of Louisville's most popular breweries and distilleries so he would have an idea of what Teller and Bat were up against. They observed them all from outside, rather than going in.

"If we do that," McCall said, "we'll be dead drunk before dusk."

"Then let's not do that," Clint said. "I'd like to eat supper by dusk."

So when dusk came, they found their way to the café across the street from The Shamrock.

"What about your hotel dining room?" McCall asked.

"I was warned away from there when it comes to supper," Clint told him.

"Warned by who?"

"By a waiter in the hotel," Clint said. "Apparently, they have a different cook for supper, and he's not nearly as good as the breakfast cook."

So they got a table in the café and ate supper there. When they stepped out, intending to cross over to the Shamrock, they saw the women from the WCTU in front.

"Who're all those women?" McCall asked.

"It's the Women's Christian Temperance League."

"What the hell is that?"

"A bunch of women who want to teach men that drinking is wicked."

"Really?" McCall said. "So let's go get wicked."

They crossed the street and as they approached the Shamrock the women barred their way.

"Sin and wickedness awaits you inside—oh," Milly said, recognizing Clint, "it's you!" She looked at McCall. "Is he persuading you to sin, sir?"

"Oh, no, lady," McCall said, with a laugh, "I found my way there a long time ago."

"Milly," the pretty Gretchen said, "let them pass."

"Sure, sure," the older woman said, "I'll let them pass." She stepped aside.

"I'm sorry, sir," Gretchen said.

"No need for you to apologize, Miss," Clint said. "You're doing something you believe in."

"Thank you," she said.

He followed McCall inside.

The bar was crowded, but Clint and McCall were able to easily make room for themselves, and were greeted by Barney.

"What can I get ya both?" the bartender asked.

"That depends," McCall said. "Are my drinks still free?"

"That was just temporary, Mad," Barney said.

"Then beer."

"Two," Clint said.

When they each had their beer Clint asked McCall, "Does it bother you when people call you 'Mad?' "

"Naw," McCall said. "Does it bother you when they call you the Gunsmith?"

"It used to," Clint said, "but then I realized there was nothing I could do about it."

"Same here," McCall said. "Why fight it? Besides, I know I don't get mad that easy."

"Oh," Clint said, remembering the look in McCall's eyes earlier, "okay."

"I think I'm gonna play some blackjack," McCall said.

"No poker?" Clint asked.

"Not my game," McCall said. "I'll keep an eye on you."

"Thanks."

McCall went to the blackjack table and took a seat. Before long there were enough people between them that Clint couldn't see him. Luckily, in spite of the fact that someone was looking for him, he didn't feel there was a need for McCall to watch his back.

Yet.

Clint was working on a second beer when he saw Boudreau come down the stairs and start to circulate through the room. He stopped at a few tables to exchange pleasantries, then walked to the bar to join Clint.

"Another one, on the house?" he asked.

"Sure, why not?"

"Two, Barney," Boudreau said.

"Right, boss."

When they each had a fresh beer Boudreau asked, "Mad McCall find you?"

"He did," Clint said. "Thanks."

"He give you some idea what Masterson wants with you?" the saloon owner asked.

"That's just it," Clint said. "He doesn't know, either."

"Then why did he put the two of you together?"

"We're waiting for Bat to get here to find that out," Clint said.

"Whataya gonna do in the meantime?"

"I'm trying to figure that out."

"I think I can help," Boudreau said.

"Oh yeah? How?"

"There's any number of gamblers in town who'd like to sit down at a poker table across from Clint Adams. I can arrange it."

"I don't think so, Mr. Boudreau," Clint said. "I'm a little out of practice. I'd be throwing my money away."

"I don't think it'll take you that long to get back to your top game," Boudreau said. "I'd be happy to back you. I'm talking about big money."

"Let me give it some thought, and I'll get back to you," Clint said.

"That's fine."

Boudreau started to turn away, but Clint stopped him.

"Let me ask you something."

"What's that?" the saloon owner asked.

"When Bat was in town, did you put games together for him?" Clint asked.

"I have."

"What about the game he was in when he won half of a local distillery?"

"That didn't happen in one of my games," Boudreau said. "I'd remember."

"That makes sense," Clint said. "Thanks."

"Sure." He waved at Barney, "Have another drink, Mr. Adams."

"Speaking of drinks," Clint said, "how are you making out with the WCTU outside?"

"Those old biddies?" Boudreau said, laughing. "They haven't affected my business in any way."

"They're not all old biddies," Clint said, "but I'm glad they're not giving you much trouble."

"I'm afraid of that old battle axe, but other than that, no trouble. Enjoy your drinks."

Chapter Sixteen

After Boudreau left and Barney gave Clint another beer, McCall came walking over, looking crestfallen.

"How'd you do?"

"Not good," McCall said. "I hate losin' to twenty-one all the time."

"That's why I don't play blackjack. Hey, Barney, set another one up."

"Sure thing, Mr. Adams."

Barney gave McCall another beer.

"Thanks," McCall said. "What was on Boudreau's mind?"

"Just wondering what was going on," Clint said.

"What'd you tell 'im?"

"Nothing, because there's nothing to tell."

"We still gotta figure out what to do while we wait for Bat to get here."

"McCall—"

"You can call me Mad," McCall said. "No problem."

"Okay, Mad," Clint said, "what would you be doing if I wasn't in Louisville?"

"Hmm," McCall said, "I'd probably be drinkin', only not here. And not alone."

"You're not alone."

McCall laughed.

"I mean a lady."

"Oh. Well, there are girls here."

"Like I said," McCall said. "Not here."

"Then where?"

"Someplace not so nice as this," McCall said.

"And the girls?"

"Also, not so nice."

"Why don't you show me?"

"Really?" McCall asked. "You can drink here and you want to go where I drink?"

"Why not?"

"Well, okay," McCall said, "but let's finish these first."

Clint finished his beer and put the mug down with a bang.

"I'm done."

McCall's mug was almost full, but he tilted it up and drained it, slapping the empty down hard.

"Let's go."

Once again they passed the women of the WCTU on the way out and fielded a murderous glance from Milly.

"I hope these women don't show up where we're go-in'," McCall said.

"I think they've got a bigger target in mind," Clint said.

***

They mounted their horses and Mad McCall led to a much different part of town. Instead of men inside saloons whooping and hollering, they were also doing it in the streets. An occasional shot rang out, but with no bad intentions.

"This reminds me of the Barbary coast, in San Francisco," Clint said.

"Ain't never been there," McCall said. "In fact, I ain't never been outside of Kentucky."

"You seem to have everything you need here," Clint said.

"And more," McCall said. "Over there, that's my favorite place."

Clint saw a dirty doorway with a rusty sign over it that actually said THE RUSTY NAIL SALOON.

"Looks interesting," he said.

They rode up to the front, dismounted and tied off their horses. When they went inside Clint saw what McCall meant by "not so nice."

Chapter Seventeen

The place was noisy and crowded, the lighting dim. Girls working the floor were scantily clad and loud. All the men, at tables and at the bar, were also loud.

McCall led the way to the bar, where men parted to leave room for the big man and his friend.

"Hey, Mad!" the bartender shouted. "Where you been?"

"Around town," McCall said. "Meet my friend Clint. Clint, this is Rod, the best bartender in town."

"Pleased to meetcha," Rod said. "Whataya you boys have?"

"Two beers, Rod."

"Drinkin' beer tonight?"

"Tryin' to stay sober for a bit."

"I don't know what fer," Rod said, "but all right."

He drew two beers and set them down with a "There ya go."

"Thanks," McCall said.

Rod went down the bar to serve some other loud customers.

"Mad!" a woman's voice called out.

Clint and McCall both turned. A once pretty, now hard-bitten woman in her thirties was approaching quickly, a big smile on her face.

"Where've you been?" she asked, throwing her arms around McCall.

"I been busy, babe," he said.

"Too busy for little Holly?"

"I'm afraid it's my fault," Clint said to Holly. "I've been keeping Mad from his usual haunts."

"Then what are ya doin' here?" she asked McCall. "Showin' your good-lookin' friend the low life?"

"That's what he asked for."

"Well," she said, removing her arms from around McCall's neck, "maybe I should show him the place."

"Why don't you?" McCall asked. "His name's Clint and if you're gonna be on his arm, it should be his left."

"No problem," she said, linking her arm in Clint's left. "Come on, honey, I'll introduce you around."

Clint allowed her to tug him off into the crowded saloon, leaving his beer on the bar so that his right hand was free.

McCall turned back to the bar and Rod came over.

"What's the gag, Mad?"

"Whataya mean?"

"You know what I meant," the bartender said "That's the Gunsmith. What's he doin' with you?"

"I'm lookin' after him for a friend," McCall said. "How do you know 'im?"

"I saw him in Abilene a few years ago," Rod said. "Outdrew three yahoos in the street. I never saw nothin' so fast."

"Is that so?"

"Is he here lookin' for somebody?"

"A friend."

"That ain't what I meant," Rod said. "We don't want any trouble in here."

"Are you kiddin'?" McCall asked. "This place ain't nothin' without trouble."

"Not the Gunsmith kind of trouble."

"You don't gotta worry about that," McCall told him. "Unless somebody else recognizes him and tries 'im."

"I hope I can count on you if that happens," the bartender said. "I don't wanna get fired."

"Frank wouldn't fire you, Rod," McCall said. "Don't worry. I'm watchin' his back."

"Watch 'im good, Mad."

"Don't worry, Holly's got him. You know she's always got a derringer in her garter."

"And she's never used it," Rod said. "Let's hope it stays that way."

Rod moved on down the bar, again.

McCall turned and looked around, saw Holly holding onto Clint, and talking with one of the other girls, Marla . . .

***

"Marla's the number two girl in the place," Holly told Clint.

Marla, a pretty little blonde who had seen better days, smiled at Clint and said, "That means Holly's number one, or so she thinks."

"Come on, Clint," Holly said. "Let's walk around some more."

She stopped occasionally to introduce Clint, and when she did she pressed her hip tightly to Clint's.

Eventually, she steered Clint into a corner and pinned him to the wall.

"Well, that's the place," she told him. "We could go up to my room for a while, if you like."

"That's a nice offer, Holly, but—"

"Since you're a friend of Mad's I'll give you a special price."

"Holly, no offense," Clint said, "but I never pay for sex."

She frowned.

"Never?"

He shook his head.

"That's too bad," she said, "because I can't afford to give it away."

"I understand."

"I'll take you back to Mad at the bar," Holly said.

Chapter Eighteen

Holly walked Clint back to McCall and said, "Here's your friend back."

"Thanks, honey," McCall said. "You gonna be available tonight?"

"As long as you got the price," Holly said.

"I'll see you later."

As Holly walked away Clint asked McCall, "She charges you?"

"Why not?" McCall asked. "That's her business."

"I thought you were friends."

"We are," McCall said, "but that don't mean she's gonna give it away. What happened between you two?"

"She offered to take me up to her room, but I told her I never pay for girls."

"You don't?"

"Never have."

"Well . . . I guess you don't need to," McCall said, "You're a lucky guy." McCall finished his beer. "You wanna try another place?"

"No, not tonight," Clint said. "I'm going to head back to my hotel."

"And do what?"

"Probably clean my guns."

"I'll ride back with you."

"You don't have to do that," Clint said. "You've got Holly waiting for you."

"That's okay," McCall said. "She won't be lonely. She's a very popular girl. Let's go."

They went outside, mounted up and rode back toward Clint's hotel.

***

Outside the Bluegrass Hotel McCall asked Clint, "Want me to come up with ya?"

"No, you don't have to," Clint said. "I'll be all right."

"What if somebody's waitin' in your room?"

"The clerk'll let me know if somebody went up."

"Unless they went the back way."

"Okay," Clint said, "come on up. We'll stop at the bar for a bottle."

"Sounds good."

They walked their horses back to the stable. McCall returned his loan and the holster took Clint's Tobiano back to his stall.

They went into the hotel and crossed the lobby to the desk. The clerk was different from the one who checked Clint in, an older man. Clint hadn't seen this one, before.

"Can I help you, sir?" the clerk asked.

"I'm Clint Adams. Was anybody here looking for me this afternoon?"

"No, sir, no one."

"Did you see any stranger in the lobby? Anyone go up the stairs?"

"No, sir," the clerk said, "but I don't know all the guests on sight."

"I guess not. Thanks." Clint turned to McCall. "Let's go to the bar for that bottle."

"I can bring it up to your room, sir," the clerk said. "Bourbon?"

"What else?" McCall asked.

"I'll bring it right up. Two glasses?"

"Yes," Clint said. "Thanks."

He and McCall went up the stairs and entered the room carefully. It was empty, just the way they had left it. Clint's saddlebags and rifle were in a corner.

"Have a seat," Clint said. "The bottle'll be here soon. You mind if I wash up?"

"Sure, go ahead."

The Bluegrass had modern lighting and indoor plumbing. Clint went into the water closet and washed up. He came out drying his hands on a towel.

"Why don't you have one drink and then go and see Holly," he suggested. "We can meet up in the lobby in the morning."

"Breakfast in the hotel again?"

"Sure thing."

There was a knock on the door. Still wearing his gun, Clint went to answer it. It was the desk clerk.

"Here's your bottle and glasses, sir."

Clint took them, tipped the man and said, "Thanks."

He closed the door and showed McCall the bottle.

"This any good?" he asked.

"I dunno. I never heard of it."

"Well, let's find out."

He opened the bottle and poured some into the two glasses, handing one to McCall. Clint sat on the edge of the bed and they both tasted it.

"I'm not much of a bourbon drinker," he told McCall.

"I am," McCall said, "I've had better." But he finished it, stood and set the glass on the table next to the bed.

"I guess you're okay here," he said. "I'll see you in the mornin'."

"Good night," Clint said. "Give Holly my best."

"I'm gonna be givin' her my best," McCall said, and left.

Chapter Nineteen

Griff Kendall waited at the Bluegrass Hotel for several hours before finally giving up. But as he left he went to the front desk and showed the desk clerk a wad of bills.

"Sir?"

"When Mr. Adams come in, I want you to give him this bottle," Kendall said, handing it to him. "Tell him it's compliments of the hotel."

"Yes, sir. Is that all?"

"That's it," Kendall said. "I'll be back to see him tomorrow, but don't tell 'im."

"No, sir."

"Thanks."

Kendall left the hotel and went home. He would make sure he met up with the Gunsmith the next day, to make his pitch.

***

Clint had one last sip of the bourbon and then set the bottle aside. The taste had not changed his mind about it. He still preferred beer.

He stripped down to his long johns, slipped beneath the sheets and went to sleep, his gun hanging within easy reach.

***

In the morning he washed again, dressed, strapped on his gun and went down to the lobby to meet McCall. He found the big man waiting impatiently by the front desk, making the young clerk nervous.

"Ready for breakfast?" Clint asked.

"Oh yeah, I'm ready."

"Any messages for me?" Clint asked the clerk.

"No, sir."

"Okay, thanks." He turned to McCall. "Let's go."

They went to the dining room and were seated by the same waiter, who remembered they wanted a back table.

"Coffee, sir?" the waiter asked Clint. The man chose not to look at Mad McCall.

"Yes," Clint said, "for both of us. And French Toast for me."

"Yes sir. And your guest?"

"Same as I had yesterday," McCall said. "You remember, right?"

"I remember," the waiter said, and hurried to the kitchen.

"I make everybody in this hotel nervous," McCall said. "The desk clerk, the waiter."

"I'll bet not the bartender," Clint said.

"Nobody makes bartenders nervous."

"How was Holly last night?" Clint asked.

"Holly was great," McCall said, "and so was Marla."

"Two girls?"

"Well," McCall said, "You been keepin' me busy, so I decided to double up."

"I feel like I should donate," Clint said.

"You said you don't pay for girls."

"That's right," Clint said, "not for myself. I don't mind donating for someone else."

"Well, thanks, but I have a rule, too," McCall said. "I always pay for my own pleasures."

"That's a good rule to have."

The waiter came back with their coffee and breakfast, and they both turned their attention to eating.

***

Griff Kendall entered the lobby of the Bluegrass and approached the front desk.

"Yes, sir?"

"I'm lookin for another desk clerk, older than you," he said.

"Oh, that'd be Orville," the young clerk said. "He left a couple of hours ago. Can I help you?"

"I'm looking for Mr. Clint Adams' room."

"We don't give out that information, sir," the clerk said, "but if you want to talk to Mr. Adams, he's in the dining room having breakfast."

"He is? Thanks." Kendall started away, then stopped. "How will I know him?"

"You won't be able to miss him," the clerk said. "He's sitting with another man—a very big man with shaggy black hair and black stubble. I don't mind telling you, he's a scary looking fellow."

"Okay, thanks."

Kendall walked to the entrance to the dining room and looked in. Quickly, he spotted the scary looking man the clerk had described. He was a decidedly rough looking character. Kendall was glad to see the man seated across from him was clean-shaven and rather good-looking. His face would look just fine on a bottle label.

He walked across the floor to their table.

Chapter Twenty

"Mr. Adams?"

Clint looked up from his plate.

"Yes?"

"Sir, my name is Griff Kendall."

"Is that supposed to mean something to me?" Clint asked.

"No, sorry," the man said. "I'd like to talk to you, if it's okay with you and your friend. May I sit?"

"It's okay with me if it's all right with my friend," Clint said.

"Okay with me," McCall said. "I'm just gonna keep on eatin'."

"Sure, no problem," the man said. He pulled a chair out and sat.

"My name's Griffin Kendall I own a local distillery here in Louisville."

Clint stopped chewing.

"Wait a minute," he said. "I saw that name on a bottle I bought last night."

McCall stopped chewing long enough to say, "Say, that's right. That was the name on the label of that bottle the clerk brought us."

"Right," Kendall said. "I paid the clerk to bring it to you."

"I asked the clerk to get me a bottle from the bar and bring it up," Clint said.

"Well, I left it with him. Maybe he brought that one up and didn't go to the bar."

"Maybe. Tell me, why'd you have him bring it to me?"

"I wanted you to taste it."

"Why would you want that? And how did you know I was even here?"

"Word gets around when somebody like the Gunsmith comes to town."

"Wait," Clint said, "were you here before, looking for me?"

"I had a friend of mine checking hotels after I heard you were in town. He finally located you here."

"So you decided to leave me a bottle?"

"I came here looking for you yesterday, but you weren't here. So I left the bottle, and came back this mornin'. Did you taste it? Did you taste my bourbon?"

When Clint hesitated, McCall said, "Yeah, we tasted it."

"What'd you think?"

"I'm not a bourbon drinker," Clint said.

"I am," McCall put in.

"Oh? What'd you think?"

McCall shrugged and said, "I've had better."

Kendall turned to face him.

"Who are you?"

"My name's McCall."

"Mad McCall?"

"You heard of me?"

"You're local."

"Yup."

"He's a friend of mine," Clint said, "I trust his opinion."

Kendall was suddenly very wary of McCall, having heard his reputation.

"Mr. Adams," he said, "I'd like to invite you to my distillery. If you didn't like the bottle I sent you, you might like something else."

"Well," Clint said, "I told you I'm not much of a bourbon drinker. Why do you want my opinion?"

"Well, I was sorta hopin' we could do some business together."

"What kind of business?"

"I was thinkin' of maybe takin' on a partner," Kendall said. "Maybe you'd be interested?"

Clint looked across the table at McCall, who simply shrugged.

"Well," Clint said, "I'm going to be around for at least a week."

"And you could use something to do durin' that time, right?"

"Something like that."

"Well, just come by and taste a few of my other barrels. And I also have beer."

"I wouldn't mind tasting the beer," Clint said.

"I hope the beer's better than the bourbon," McCall said.

"That was just one bottle, Mr. McCall," Kendall said. "I'm sure I have somethin' you'd like."

McCall looked at Clint.

"I wouldn't mind tastin' some."

"Sure, why not?" Clint asked.

"Excellent," Kendall said happily. "You could come by this afternoon and I'll have something ready for you."

"Sure," Clint said, "where's your place?"

"I'll give you the address."

"Tell Mr. McCall," Clint said. "Since he's local, he'll get me there."

Kendall gave McCall the address, then stood up.

"I'll leave you gentlemen to your breakfast, now," he said, "and see you both later. And thank you."

Chapter Twenty-One

After Kendall left the dining room, Clint looked at McCall and asked, "What do you think?"

"I toldja," McCall said, "I've had better, but you're just lookin' for a way to pass the time, so why not taste?"

"Sure, why not?"

"But first I want some more of this," McCall said, and waved at the waiter . . .

***

After they finished breakfast, they left the hotel and went to the livery. There were horse drawn cabs available on the street of Louisville, but neither Clint nor McCall wanted to be dependent on someone else to get them where they wanted to go.

Clint waited outside with his Tobiano, til McCall came out with the same horse he had the day before.

As they rode away from the hotel Clint asked McCall, "So if you've never been out of Kentucky, how often do you ride?"

"There are plenty of places in Kentucky to ride to," the big man said.

"Then why don't you own a horse?"

"There's no sense payin' board for an animal I hardly use," McCall replied. "I just as soon borrow or rent one when the time comes. Then I can spend the rest of my money on whiskey and women."

"How much money do you spend on those things?" Clint asked.

"Not much," McCall said. "I'm satisfied with cheap whiskey and sad women."

"I never asked you what you do for money?" Clint said.

"Odd jobs," McCall said. "And I only do 'em when I need the money."

"You seem to have your life all figured out," Clint said.

"I'm fifty-years-old, and it took me a while, but yeah, I do."

"Have you got many friends?"

"Sure I do," McCall said, "I got you and Bat."

"And Holly," Clint added."

"McCall laughed and said, "Sure, as long as I pay her."

***

Clint got an idea and decided to send a telegram before going to Griff Kendall's distillery. He asked McCall to take him to a telegraph office.

As they dismounted in front of it McCall asked, "What's on your mind."

"The telegrams I got from Bat sounded odd," Clint said, "so I decided to check them out. After all, you really can't tell who sends a telegram. You've got to trust they're being sent by the right person."

"So whataya gonna do?"

"I've got a friend in Denver who can look into it for me," Clint said. "And if it was Bat, my friend can also check on his condition."

"You think somebody's pretendin' to be Bat?"

"I just want to be sure," Clint said. "The first couple of telegrams, the one that brought me here, sounded legitimate. I mean, they sent me to you and Boudreau. But the one about him being shot, and the one that told me to be patient . . . like I said. I'm just checking."

Inside, Clint wrote out a telegram to his friend, Talbot Roper, asking him to confirm that Masterson had been shot, but was alright.

Outside the telegraph office Clint said, "We should have a reply by the time we get back to my hotel."

"Who's this Roper, fella?" McCall asked, as they mounted up.

"Only the best private detective in the country."

"Better than the Pinkertons?" McCall asked.

"Much better."

They headed off at an easy pace to the Kendall distillery.

***

When they reined in their horses in front of the building it wasn't in the neighborhood that Ben Teller and Bat's place was, but the building looked every bit as solid. The sign over the door said:

KENDALL DISTILLERY AND BREWERY.

They dismounted and tied off their mounts.

"He might be surprised we're here so early," Clint said.

"I like keepin fellers off balance," McCall said. "This feller had an edge to him. I ain't so sure about him, and like I said, I've tasted better."

"Well, let's see how he reacts."

They found the metal front door locked, so Clint pounded his fist on it . . .

***

Griff Kendall had rushed back to the distillery from the Bluegrass Hotel. He expected Clint Adams at his place in the afternoon, but he wanted to be ready for anything. And he almost was, by the time Clint and McCall arrived and banged on his door.

Chapter Twenty-Two

"Come on in!" Kendall greeted. "You're early."

"Is that a problem?" Clint asked.

"Not at all. You and your buddy are welcome. Follow me."

Kendall closed the door, locked it and took the lead.

"Why lock the door?" Clint asked.

"There've been some break-ins around here, lately," Kendall explained.

"Lose some money?" McCall asked.

"No," Kendall said, "looks like the thieves were lookin' for formulas."

He took them down a hall and into a large room full of vats. Against the far wall was a table filled with bottles.

"I thought we'd try some bourbon first," Kendall said. "Then I'll draw some beer."

"It's your call," Clint said.

"Try this one."

Kendall opened a bottle and poured them each a glass. Clint took a sip, but didn't have the palate to tell if it was any good so he simply nodded.

McCall took a healthy swig from his glass and looked thoughtful.

"Well?" Kendall asked.

"Let's try another one," McCall said.

Kendall frowned and opened another bottle. He handed them each a glass and they repeated the process, a small sip from Clint, and a large gulp for McCall.

"Well?" Kendall asked, again.

"Maybe it's a bad batch," McCall said.

"And maybe you don't know good bourbon," Kendall said, getting his back up.

"You don't want to get my friend mad, do you, Mr. Kendall?" Clint asked. "Maybe he just doesn't like your stuff."

"My stuff is damned good, Mr. Adams," Kendall said, "With your name on the label—"

"What?"

"Gunsmith Bourbon," Kendall said. "Whataya think?"

"I think we're done here," Clint said.

"But you haven't tasted the beer," Kendall said.

"And we're not going to," Clint said. "Thanks for the samples, Mr. Kendall, but I'm not interested."

"Maybe you would be if it wasn't for your friend, here," Kendall said.

Clint saw a glint in Mad McCall's eyes.

"I think we better leave before you get my friend mad, Kendall."

"I'll take you to the door," Kendall huffed.

He walked briskly ahead of them and unlocked the door well before they caught up.

"Maybe we can talk about this again, Mr. Adams?" Kendall asked.

"I don't think so, Mr. Kendall," Clint said. "I'm really not interested in putting my name on your label."

"It'd make us a lot of money!" Kendall insisted. "Come on, give it a little more thought."

"No amount of thought is gonna change the taste, Clint," McCall said. "Come on, let's go someplace and get a real drink. I'll show you some good stuff." McCall looked at Kendall. "See ya again some time."

He and Clint walked out the door, and Kendall slammed it behind them.

"I think we hurt his feelings," Clint said, as they mounted up. "I'd say you were right."

"About what?" McCall asked.

"You don't get mad so easy."

"I told you!"

***

Kendall stormed back to his office, threw himself into his chair and poured himself a drink. He gulped down half of it and couldn't see what Mad McCall had against it. The stuff was first rate.

He decided not to give up so easy. All he had to do was get Clint Adams away from Mad McCall and make a fresh pitch.

***

McCall took Clint to a saloon called The Stackhouse.

"McCall!" the bartender greeted. "Where the hell ya been, Mad?"

"I been around, Harry," McCall said. "This is my friend, Clint Adams."

"Nice to meet you, Mr. Adams," the bartender said. "I think I know that name."

"You do, Harry," McCall said, "but let's keep it quiet, huh?"

"Sure, Mad, sure. What can I getcha?"

"I want to show Clint what good bourbon tastes like. Set 'em up!"

Chapter Twenty-Three

Clint and McCall had a few drinks at the bar, then McCall chose a bottle to take to a table. Clint ordered a beer and took it with him.

"What do you think of this bottle?" McCall asked, pouring Clint a drink.

After taking a sip Clint said, "To tell you the truth, Mad, I can't tell the difference between this and what we had at Kendall's."

"And how's that beer?"

"This? Real good."

"You're right, it is," McCall said. "So you just don't have a taste for bourbon, good or bad."

"Mad, I'm not much of a whiskey drinker. But I also don't appreciate wine or champagne. I'm a beer drinker."

"Well, I'm sure Kendall would put your picture on his beer," McCall said.

"Not a chance," Clint said. "I don't like the idea that he was already planning the whole thing ahead of time."

"I knew I didn't like him from the minute I saw him," McCall said.

"Neither did I," Clint said. "I was just looking for something to do."

"Well, we wasted some time." McCall poured himself another drink.

"I wonder how deep Bat's going to get into the distillery business?" Clint asked. "His picture on a label would sell a lot of bourbon."

"You really think Bat would go for that?" McCall asked.

"Actually no," Clint said. "Bat would be more likely to put his picture on a deck of cards."

McCall raised his eyebrows.

"Now that sounds like a good idea," he said. "Would you go for that?"

Clint laughed. "Not a chance."

"Well," McCall said, "whataya wanna do now?"

"Get back to my hotel, I guess," Clint said. "See if there's a telegram."

"Okay," McCall said, "let's go."

As they walked past the bar McCall said, "See ya, Harry."

"Don't stay away so long, Mad," the bartender said.

Clint and McCall went out the front door. As they started to mount up, there was a shot, and Clint heard McCall grunt. Turning, he saw the big man slumping to the ground. He took a quick look around, then rushed to McCall's side.

"Mad? Where are you hit?"

"My back, my back . . ." McCall groaned.

"Let me take a look," Clint said.

He rolled McCall over, and saw a bloody hole high up on the right side of his back.

A couple of men came running out of the saloon, followed by Harry, the bartender.

"How is he?" Harry asked.

"He's alive," Clint said. "Get a doctor."

"Right."

"Clint . . . get 'im . . ." McCall said, trying to stand up.

"Stay down, Mad," Clint said. "There'll be a doctor here soon."

"Go, Clint," McCall said. "Find 'im."

There was a crowd around them, now. Clint stood up.

"Anybody see anything?" he asked.

"I thought I saw a guy run into that alley across the street," somebody said.

"Stay with him," Clint snapped. "Make sure he doesn't get up."

He ran across the street to the alley and into it. It was dark, but there was light at the end. He took the chance and ran headlong up to the other side. When he came out, he looked both ways and saw no one. He went back down the alley, checked the ground, then went back across the street to where McCall was lying.

"Mad?" he said, crouching down next to him.

"Clint? You get 'im?"

"No, he got away."

Harry appeared, with an older man in tow.

"This is Doc Fairlie," the bartender said.

The doctor crouched down next to McCall.

"Turn him over, please," he said.

Clint took McCall by the shoulders and turned him over carefully. The doctor examined the wound as best he could.

"How bad, Doc?" Clint asked.

"Hard to tell here," Fairlie said. "I need to get him to my office."

"Where is it?" Clint asked.

"Just down the street."

Clint looked at Harry.

"Let's get him carried there."

"Right," Harry said. "Come on, a few of you guys carry 'im."

Four men came forward, gathered around McCall and lifted him up.

"Follow me," Doc Fairlie said, and led the way.

Chapter Twenty-Four

When Doctor Fairlie got McCall into his examination room, Harry and the other men left while Clint sat in the waiting area. After about half-an-hour the doctor came out.

"How is he?" Clint asked.

"He'll be all right," the doctor said. "The bullet hit him high on the right side, so it's not near his heart."

"Did you get it out?"

"I did, but it took some digging," the doctor said. "It'll take a while for him to recover, but he's big and he's very strong."

"Can he be moved?"

"I want keep him here for a few days," Fairlie said. "After that he can be moved. You could take him home."

"I'm going to take him to my hotel, get him a room," Clint said.

"It'd be good to have somebody watch him," Fairlie said. "If I had a nurse—"

"I can get a girl to watch him," Clint said, thinking of Holly.

"That'll be good," Fairlie said.

"Can I see him?" Clint asked.

"Not for long," Fairlie said. "He needs his rest."

Clint went into the next room. McCall was lying on a table, covered by a sheet. When Clint entered, McCall tuned his head.

"Hey, Clint," he groaned.

"Mad," Clint said, approaching the table. "Did you see anything?"

"No, not a thing," McCall said. "I heard the shot, then felt the lead. I been shot before, so I knew it wasn't too bad. The doc tells me I was right, I'll be off my feet for a while but will be able to go home soon."

"I know," Clint said. "I'm going to put you in my hotel, Mad, in your own room."

"Is the hotel gonna go for that?"

"They will, because I'm going to pay."

"Hey, Clint—"

"Don't argue," Clint said. "I'm going to get Holly to stay with you."

"Holly? She's got a job—"

"I'm going to pay for her, too," Clint said. "I'm not sure that bullet wasn't meant for me."

"If that's true, the guy was a bad shot. What makes you think that?"

"I don't want to say I've gotten used to being shot at, but it happens."

"I know, it happens to me, too, so it could've been meant for either one of us."

"True enough."

The door opened and Doctor Fairlie came in.

"That's enough, Mister . . ."

"Adams," Clint said. "Okay." He looked at McCall. "I'll be back tomorrow."

"Okay, Clint," McCall said. "Meantime, watch your back. If that shot was meant for you, they might try again."

"I'll be careful," Clint said. "I'm going to go see Holly, and then get back to my hotel. But we'll need somebody to watch your back while you're in bed. Is there anybody?"

"Go and see Harry," McCall said. "He'll give you somebody."

"Mr. Adams . . ." Fairlie said.

"I'm going, Doc, I'm going . . ."

***

Clint left the doctor's office and walked back to the Stackhouse Saloon.

"How's McCall?" Harry asked, when he saw Clint.

"The doc says he'll be all right, but he's going to need rest."

"At doc's?"

"I'm going to put him someplace safe," Clint said.

"You think the shooter's gonna try again?"

"He might," Clint said. "Then again I might've been the target."

"How are you gonna find out?"

"I'm going to look," Clint said. "Meanwhile, I'm going to need somebody to watch McCall. He told me you could get me somebody."

"I know a couple of guys who'd do it," Harry said. "I can have 'em here tomorrow."

"That's good," Clint said. "Tomorrow morning?"

"Afternoon," Harry said. "That's the fastest I can get 'em."

"Okay," Clint said. "I'm going to stop in tomorrow and see McCall. Then I'll come here."

"Is he gonna be safe tonight?"

"Probably," Clint said. "I don't think they'll try again with the doc there."

"Okay," Harry said, "then I'll see you tomorrow."

"Right," Clint said and left.

Chapter Twenty-Five

Clint managed to get back to his hotel room without anyone taking a shot at him. The night desk clerk gave him a telegram that had been delivered during the day. It was from Talbot Roper and confirmed that Bat Masterson had, indeed, been shot and was spending time in a Denver hospital. Roper also confirmed that the telegrams Clint had received from Bat were legitimate.

In his room Clint gave some thought to Bat Masterson and Mad McCall both being shot from ambush. Bat could have been shot by someone looking for a reputation. Clint was going to send another telegram to Talbot Roper asking the detective to look into the matter in Denver. Clint knew Masterson would want to investigate the matter himself, but by the time he got out of the hospital, the trail might have gone cold.

As for Kentucky, the shot could actually have been meant for Mad McCall. After all, the man had a reputation there. But Clint's reputation was far more widespread. It seemed likely to him that he was the intended target, and McCall was hit by accident.

In any case, he was still going to pay for someone to keep watch over McCall, and for Holly to look after him while he stayed in the Bluegrass Hotel. Both McCall and Holly would enjoy a stay in the hotel, with lots of room service.

With Mad McCall safely ensconced in the hotel, Clint would be able to spend his time trying to find out who the shooter was.

Back in his own room he took steps to be sure he was safe. He jammed a chair under the doorknob to be sure the locked door stayed closed. There was no access to the room from outside the window. As always, his gun was hanging nearby, so Clint was able to get a decent night's sleep.

In the morning he had another fine breakfast in the dining room before sending another telegram to Talbot Roper in Denver. But before he could get to it, a man approached his table before he finished his meal.

"Mr. Adams?"

"That's right."

"I'm Detective Pitkin of the Louisville Police Department. Can we talk?"

"About what?"

"A shooting that took place last night. The victim was Mad McCall?"

"Sure," Clint said. "Have a seat."

The detective pulled out a chair and sat across from Clint.

"We heard you were there when McCall was shot," Pitkin said.

"Heard from who?" Clint asked.

"I talked with Mad McCall earlier this morning," the policeman said. "He said you both came out of the Stackhouse, and there was a shot."

"That's right."

"Do you think there's a chance you were the intended victim?"

"I think there's a good chance, Detective," Clint said. "That's why I'm going to look into it."

"Do you think you can do my job?"

"I think with both of us looking into it, maybe we'll find the shooter."

"Do you have any idea who it was?" Pitkin asked.

"No, not yet," Clint said. "First I have to decide who the target was, McCall or me."

"You both have reputations," Pitkin said. "You think somebody was looking for a reputation maker?"

"Could be."

"Well then, it would make more sense for you to be the target."

"Doesn't McCall have a name in Louisville?"

"Nothing like yours," Pitkin said, standing up. "As far as my chief is concerned, you were the target."

"Okay," Clint said. "You go on that assumption."

"I'll want you both to stay where I can find you," the lieutenant said. "And let me know where you'll be."

"I'll be here," Clint said. "And I'll find a place for McCall."

"All right," Pitkin said, "but keep me informed."

"I will."

"It was nice to meet you, Mr. Adams."

The policeman left the dining room, and Clint finished his breakfast. The detective was a stranger to him, which was why Clint didn't tell him that McCall was going to be in the hotel. That information he wanted to keep to himself.

He left the hotel and went to the telegraph office.

***

After he sent the telegram to Talbot Roper in Denver, he stopped at Doctor Fairlie's.

"Yeah, Pitkin stopped in here early," McCall said. "He woke me up."

"So he's on the level?" Clint asked. "He's a local policeman?"

"Yeah, why?" McCall asked.

"He wants to know where we're going to be," Clint said. "I didn't tell him you'll be in the Bluegrass."

"Playin' it safe, huh?" McCall asked. "That's smart, butya don't gotta worry about Pitkin. He's part of Louisville's new police department."

"Okay, then," Clint said. "We'll stick with the plan and put you in the hotel. I'm going to the Stackhouse from here to see who Harry's got for us."

"It's gotta be somebody good," McCall said. "Just don't let him give ya Dave Burroughs."

"Why not?"

"He ain't reliable."

"Why would Harry try to give him to us?"

"Dave's his brother-in-law," McCall said. "Harry's sister's always tryin' to get Harry to give Dave a job. I don't want his job to be tryin' to keep me alive."

"Got it," Clint said. "No Dave Burroughs."

"You talk to Holly, yet?"

"No," Clint said, "I'll do that after I talk to Harry."

"Okay," McCall said. "So when do I get moved into your hotel?"

"I'll get it all set up for tomorrow," Clint said. "I'll come and get you myself."

"Suits me," McCall said. "This doc is keepin' me in when I want to get out."

"The hotel won't be much better," Clint said. "I'm going to keep you in until you heal."

Chapter Twenty-Six

From the doctor's office Clint went to the Stackhouse Saloon.

"Harry," he said, at the bar, "you got anything for me?"

"I got a couple of men, Mr. Adams," Harry said. "they're sittin' over there. Come on."

Clint put his hand out to stop Harry.

"One of them isn't named Burroughs, is he?"

"Hell, no," Harry said, "I wouldn't trust Mad McCall's life to my idiot brother-in-law. Come on."

He walked Clint over to the two men at the table. It was early, and there weren't many other customers in the place.

"Clint Adams, this is Hal Wilkes and Buck Olson. They both know Mad McCall. I'll get you all fresh beers."

As Harry went to the bar Wilkes said, "Siddown, Mr. Adams. Harry told us what you need."

"We're happy to take the job," Olson said.

"Are you both friends of McCall's?"

"Hell, no," Wilkes said. "Mad McCall doesn't have any friends. We're just happy to take the job and keep 'im alive."

"Why? If you're not friends?"

"We don't like bushwhackers," Olson said.

"And we're for hire," Wilkes added.

"So just tell us where and when," Olson said, "and we'll be there."

***

After talking with Wilkes and Olson, Clint went to The Rusty Nail to see Holly.

"Everything okay?" Rod asked.

"Fine," Clint said, "I'd like to talk to Holly."

"Oh, that's it," Rod said. "She's up in her room."

"Asleep?"

"Probably not. She's an early riser, but she needs time to, you know, fix her face. She ain't as young as she used to be."

"Can I go up?"

"Sure," Rod said. "Just make sure you knock."

"I will."

"Top of the stairs," Rod said.

"Thanks."

Clint went up the stairs and knocked on the door. When it opened Holly was standing there, wearing a rather worn out silk robe. Without makeup she looked closer to forty than thirty.

"Well, well," Holly said, "look who's here. It's a little early, isn't it?"

"That's what the bartender said," Clint said. "I'm not here for the usual reasons, Holly."

"Really? That's a shame. I was hopin' second thoughts brought you up here."

"I'm afraid not," Clint said. "The reason I'm here is Mad McCall."

"McCall?" Holly said. "Well, come on in and tell me about it."

"Were you here last night?"

"No," she said, "I had the night off. Why?"

"There was a shooting in front of the Stackhouse Saloon last night," Clint said.

"I know that place. Who got shot?"

"McCall."

She looked alarmed.

"What? Is he dead?"

"No," Clint said, "but he's going to be laid up for a while."

"Poor Mad." Then she frowned. "So why are you here?"

"I'm putting Mad in a room in my hotel," Clint said, "but he'll need a nurse."

"You want me to recommend somebody?" she asked. "The girls I know ain't exactly nurse types."

"Well, you're friends with Mad," Clint said. "I was hoping you'd see you're way clear to doing it."

"What, me? Be a nurse?"

"Not so much nurse, as nursemaid," Clint said. "I'll get you a room in the hotel, and you just keep an eye on him. Maybe have some room service meals together."

"At the Bluegrass?"

"That's the place."

"That's quite a hotel."

"Yes, it is."

"What about my job?"

"Oh, I intend to pay you. How much do you want?"

She got a thoughtful look on her face.

"Maybe we can talk about that later," she said. "But now you can give me a down payment."

"Sure thing," Clint said. "What'd you have in mind?"

"Well . . ." She undid the belt on her robe and opened it, revealing herself to be naked underneath. Clint had noticed the large nipples poking little hills in the silk, and assumed she slept in the nude and slipped the robe on when he knocked.

"Now Holly—"

"Huh-uh," she said, dropping the robe to the floor. "This is part of the deal."

She moved close enough to Clint for him to feel the heat from her body. Although she was a faded looking saloon girl, she was also extremely sexy. She unbuttoned his shirt and ran her knowing hands over his bare chest . . .

Chapter Twenty-Seven

After peeling off Clint's shirt, she dropped her hands to his belt. He reached down and grabbed her by the wrists.

"Easy, lover," she said. "I'm not after your gun, just your pants."

"Part of the deal?" he asked.

"Definitely."

"Well then," he said, "let me help."

He undid his gunbelt and set it aside within easy reach.

"Okay," he said, spreading his arms, "but first let's lock the door."

She stepped past him, and he watched her lock the door. He could see there was a time when Holly had been a young beauty. Now her body had some extra weight on it around the waist and her bottom, but she was still sexy as hell.

She turned around and pressed her back to the door.

"Now let's get those clothes off . . ."

***

When they were naked together on the bed, she got him on his back, then crawled down between his legs. She kissed his thighs and licked his penis until she had him good and hard, then took him into her mouth. She sucked him until he was thoroughly wet, then climbed aboard and slid him into her hot, wet pussy and rode like a wild woman . . .

***

"Jesus," Clint breathed, while he dressed.

"Did I wear you out?" she asked, lying on her back, stretched out, fully nude. Her large breasts were flattened out by their weight, and yet she was still the picture of sex.

"You wore me out, for sure," Clint said, buttoning his shirt.

"When do you want me to start as Mad's nurse?" she asked.

"I'll have him in the Bluegrass sometime tomorrow," he answered, "so tomorrow afternoon would be good. If you come to the hotel, there'll be a room waiting for you."

He grabbed his gunbelt and strapped it on.

She rolled over onto her left side, both breasts falling that way.

"Before you leave, we better talk money," she said. "After all, *I am* a workin' girl."

"I know that," Clint said.

"And so does Mad," she assured him, "but *I am* happy to look after him."

"Okay," he said, "let's talk money . . ."

***

When Clint came back down, he got a knowing look from Rod.

"How'd it go?" Rod called out.

Clint was going to walk right out, but he changed direction and went to the bar.

"Holly's going to do a job for me," Clint said. "I hope that won't get her in trouble with your boss."

"Hell no," Rod said. "Holly's worked here long enough to make her own rules."

"That's good to hear."

"Just out of curiosity, what's the job?" Rod asked.

"I hired her to be a nurse, in case your boss asks you."

Rod laughed.

"A nurse? To who?"

"Mad McCall."

"Mad got hurt? Is he—"

"He's okay. He got shot, but he's alive. He needs rest and somebody to care for him. Holly took the job."

"I see. Who shot 'im?"

"That's what I intend to find out," Clint said. "The shot might have been meant for me, and hit McCall by mistake."

"Well, you both have reputations," Rod pointed out. "Good luck."

Chapter Twenty-Eight

Clint spent the rest of the afternoon arranging a room for McCall and one next to it for Holly. The desk clerk brought him to the owner's office. The man stood up from his desk, revealing himself to be tall, thin and very well dressed.

"Mr. Adams," the man said, "happy to have you in our hotel. My name is Victor Lourde. I'm told you need two connecting rooms in addition to your own."

"That's right," Clint said. "A friend of mine was shot and needs to rest. I can't think of a better place."

"And the other room?"

"I hired a nurse to look after him."

"Ah, I see."

"I hope this won't be a problem," Clint said. "I can pay for the rooms."

"That's not a problem," Lourde said "I'm happy to have a guest of your caliber in the hotel. Uh, no pun intended."

"I insist on paying for the rooms," Clint said, ignoring the joke.

"I'll give you a special rate, then."

"That's fine, Mr. Lourde."

"When did you want the rooms?"

"As soon as possible."

"Very well," Lourde said. "I'll have a maid get right on that."

"Thank you."

"You can bring your guest here in the morning."

"I appreciate that."

Clint left the owner's office and went back to the front desk.

"Is everything all right, sir?"

"It's all set," Clint said. "I'll be here in the morning with my guest."

"I'll make sure the rooms are ready, Mr. Adams, and as close to your room as possible."

"I appreciate that."

"Are you expecting any other telegrams, sir?"

"No," Clint said, "and I'll be out for the evening."

"Yes, sir."

Clint left the hotel, went around back to the livery to collect his horse. Something had occurred to him, and he wanted to check it out right away.

***

Clint reined in his Tobiano in front of Griff Kendall's distillery and dismounted. In wondering who might have taken a shot at Mad McCall that afternoon, he suddenly thought about Kendall. McCall's opinion of Kendall's bourbon had an effect on Clint's reaction. Maybe not as big as Kendall might have thought. Clint wanted to see Kendall's face when he put it to him.

Clint found the door locked, as before, and pounded on it. When Kendall opened it, he looked both pleased and surprised.

"You came back!" he said. "I thought you might. And I was hopin' you wouldn't bring your friend. Let me take you back—"

"Let's go to your office and talk, Kendall," Clint suggested.

"Sure, sure," Kendall said, "let's talk."

Clint followed Kendall to his office, where the man sat at his desk.

"Have a seat. Can I give you a drink?"

"No, thanks," Clint said. "I'm not here to taste anything."

"Then what brings you here?"

"Mad McCall was shot last night."

"That's too bad," Kendall said. "How is he?"

"He's alive, but he's going to be off his feet for a while."

"And why does that bring you here?"

"Did you think you might change my mind if you got a chance to see me alone? Without McCall?"

"Wait a minute," Kendall said, sitting up straight. "Do you think I shot McCall?"

"I think it's possible."

"Why would I do that?"

"To get me alone and change my mind."

"You came here on your own," Kendall said. "I didn't invite you this time."

"That's true enough," Clint said. "But that doesn't clear you."

"You can't prove anythin', either," Kendall said. "Look, I'm a businessman. I don't shoot people."

"Maybe you know somebody who does."

"You're crazy!" Kendall said. "I think you better leave. Unless you're gonna talk business."

Clint stood up.

"I don't think so," Clint said. "I'm going to find out who shot McCall. If I find out you're involved, I'll be back."

"If you keep botherin' me, I'll go to the law."

"Ask for Detective Pitkin," Clint said. "He's looking for the shooter, too."

"Go on, get out!" Kendall said. "I'll sell my stuff without you."

Chapter Twenty-Nine

When Clint left Kendall's distillery, he went to the Louisville Police Headquarters.

"Can I help you, sir?" the uniformed policeman on the front desk asked.

"I'd like to see Detective Pitkin."

"Have a seat," the man said. "I'll see if he's around."

"Thanks."

For a lot of years marshal's and sheriff's offices were the same everywhere. Now that more modern police departments were showing up all over the West—even the Midwest—they were looking the same. Clint had been to buildings like this one in New York, Chicago, St. Louis, Denver and many other cities. Even the bench he sat on to wait looked the same.

The officer on the desk hadn't asked Clint for his name, so when Pitkin came out Clint could see he didn't know who was waiting.

"Oh, Mr. Adams," he said. "They should've told me it was you. Come on back."

He led Clint through the building to an office.

"Have a seat," Pitkin said. "What's on your mind?"

"Do you know a man name Griffin Kendall?"

"Kendall? Sure, he's got a local distillery."

"What kind of guy is he?"

"His stuff isn't very good," Pitkin said. "He's more of a salesman, always lookin for an angle to work." How do you know him?"

"He made a pitch for me to put my name on his label. Gunsmith bourbon."

"Yeah, that's an angle, all right. I hope you turned him down."

"I did, but first we went to his place to taste his stuff."

"And?"

"I'm not a bourbon drinker, but McCall said he'd had better."

"How did Kendall take that?"

"Not good."

"Wait a minute," Pitkin said. "Are you thinkin' maybe Kendall shot McCall?"

"I'm thinking it's a possibility."

"Did you accuse him?"

"I went to see him today. We talked, and he told me to get out. "I don't think he's going to want my name on his label, anymore."

"Don't believe it" Pitkin said. "He'd take your name in a minute."

"It's not going to happen," Clint said. "What do you think, Detective? Would Kendall stoop that low?"

"In a minute," Pitkin said. "I'll go and have a talk with him and see if you're right. Meanwhile, you better watch your back."

"I always do," Clint said.

"And where's McCall?"

"I've got him hidden away, with two men looking out for him."

"Can you trust them?"

"I got them from somebody McCall trusts."

"Okay," Pitkin said. "Look, I'll come by your hotel after I talk to Kendall."

"Thanks, Pitkin."

"Sure." The detective stood up. "I'll walk you out."

At the front door Pitkin said, "Try to keep your head low, Mr. Adams."

"I will."

"And my chief would appreciate if you didn't kill anybody while you're in town."

"I'll give that my best try."

He mounted the Tobiano and rode back to his hotel.

***

121

After he boarded the horse in the stable he went inside. The desk clerk waved him over.

"Telegram, Mr. Adams."

"Thanks."

"And those rooms are ready," the young man said. "Right across from yours."

"That's good. Thanks. I'll bring my people over tomorrow."

"Fine."

"I'm kind of hungry," Clint said. "Is the food really bad here for supper?"

"Well, it ain't as good as breakfast," the clerk said, "but if you don't want anything fancy, you should be okay."

"Okay, then I'll be in there having a steak."

"Thanks, sir."

Sitting at the same table waiting for his steak, Clint read the telegram from Talbot Roper. It was short. Roper said he was on the case and would find out who shot Bat.

After that the steak came, he turned all his attention to it.

Chapter Thirty

The next morning Clint went to Doc Fairlie's office with a buggy. He helped McCall get dressed and walked him out. From there they went to the Rusty Nail and picked up Holly.

At the Bluegrass Clint and Holly helped McCall out of the buggy.

"I'm okay," McCall insisted. "Stop babying me."

"That's what I'm gettin' paid for, ain't it?"

Holly took the lead up the stairs, and Clint walked behind McCall. When they got him to his room, Clint helped him undress and get into bed.

"This is some room," Holly said, once McCall was in bed.

"It sure is," McCall said. "Clint, you said we could get food brought up here?"

"Sure thing."

"Then let's get some of that good breakfast," McCall said. "Holly, you're gonna love the breakfast, here."

"Great," she said. "I'm starved."

"I'll go down and take care of it," Clint said. "Wilkes and Olson should be down there eating. I'll bring them up with me."

"I know Wilkes," Holly said, "but not the other man." She looked at McCall. "I didn't know you and Wilkes were friends."

"We ain't," McCall said. "But he's a pro."

"I'll be back," Clint said. "Don't open the door for anyone, Holly. I have a key."

"Right."

"And make sure you bring up some coffee," McCall said.

"Sure thing."

Clint went down to the dining room and found Wilkes and Olson halfway through breakfast.

"You fellows all set?" he asked.

"We'll be all set when we finish here."

"Okay," Clint said. "I'm going to bring some breakfast up for McCall and Holly. I'll come and get you when I'm ready to go."

"We'll be here."

The waiter came over to Clint.

"A table, sir?"

"No, I want some breakfast to take up to the room," Clint said.

"Just tell me what you want."

"Three plates and a lot of coffee," Clint said.

"Comin' up, Mr. Adams."

"I'll be waiting at that table, with those two men."

"Gotcha."

Clint went and sat with Wilkes and Olson until the waiter came with the plates.

"Thanks."

"I can carry these up for you," the waiter offered.

"That's okay, I've got help. Come on, boys."

They each carried a plate upstairs, with Olsen taking a pot of coffee, and Wilkes some cups. Clint kept his right hand free.

***

"You were right!" Holly raved. "That was a great breakfast."

"I told you," McCall said.

McCall managed to sit up and support his plate on his lap. Holly sat with Clint at a small table that had been brought in. Wilkes and Olson were in place, one in the hall and one in the lobby.

When they were finished and all the plates had been carried away McCall said to Clint, "You ain't gonna sit in here all day, are ya?"

"No," Clint said, "I'm still looking for the shooter."

"That's good," McCall said. "Holly'll take care of me just fine."

"You betcha, honey," Holly said.

Up to this point Clint had only seen Holly in a flashy dress, a robe, and naked. Today she was wearing a simple dress that covered her to the neck, but molded itself to her curves.

"Don't get too rough with him, Holly," Clint said. "The doctor doesn't want that wound to start bleeding again."

"I'll be gentle as a lamb with him, Clint," she said. "Don't worry."

"I'll be back this afternoon, Mad," Clint said.

"No rush, Clint," McCall said. "No rush."

Clint left the room, nodded to Wilkes, and then downstairs to Olson, on the way out.

***

"I thought he'd never leave, honey," McCall said, reaching under the sheets, "Help me get these skivvies down, honey."

"I'm supposed to be takin' care of you, Mad," Holly said.

"That's just what I want you to do, babe," McCall said, "take good care of me."

"Oh, okay"

Holly went to the bed, pulled the sheet off him, and helped him pull his skivvies down. A monstrously hard cock popped up at her, and Holly not only helped McCall, but helped herself, as well . . .

Chapter Thirty-One

Clint decided to go back to the scene of the shooting, outside The Rusty Nail, to question some people from the area and see if they saw anything. All he needed was one witness. He rode there and left his horse in front of the Saloon while he walked the area. There were several shops that would have been open at the time, so Clint stopped in to talk to employees and/or owners. The only problem was, they all claimed to have not seen or heard a thing.

"One shot?" a man said. "In this neighborhood, that ain't unusual."

"I guess not."

"Who got shot?"

"A man named Mad McCall."

"I know McCall," the shop owner said.

"From where?" Clint asked.

"I usually stop into the Rusty Nail after work," the man said. "McCall spends a lot of time there."

"Has he ever been in a fight in the saloon?" Clint asked. "Maybe somebody spotted him and wanted to get back at him."

"Oh, he's been in a few scrapes," the man said, "but I never saw him involved in gunplay. Not in the saloon, anyway."

"Okay, thanks," Clint said.

The opinion of everybody he spoke to seemed to be the same. Shots in that neighborhood weren't unusual. He decided to talk to someone who might actually know something . . .

***

"Hey, how's Mad?" Rod, the bartender, asked as Clint entered the Rusty Nail and approached the bar.

"The doc said he'll be all right, but he's got to stay off his feet."

"Where is he?"

"I stashed him somewhere safe," Clint said.

"You want a beer?"

"Sure."

Rod drew a cold one and set it down in front of him.

"Let me ask you something, Rod," Clint said. "Do you know anyone who'd want to put a bullet in McCall?"

"You mean an enemy?" Rod asked. "He don't have many friends, but I don't know of anybody who wants him dead."

"Then maybe the shot was meant for me," Clint reasoned. "And Mad got in the way."

"You ain't been in town long enough to make any enemies, have you?"

"Somebody just has to recognize me and get the notion to make a try at me."

"It must be hell being that well known that somebody'd just take it into their head to try to shoot you," Rod said.

"I've learned to live with that for a lot of years."

"So even though this is McCall's town, you're thinking the shot was meant for you?"

"I only have one other idea, and so far it hasn't panned out."

"So what are you gonna do?"

"Keep looking," Clint said.

"What if somebody takes another shot?" Rod asked.

"They better know what they're doin'," Clint said, "because next time I'll be ready."

"I don't think I'd want to go up against you when you're ready,"

"McCall said you're the best bartender in town," Clint said. "Maybe you can keep your ear to the ground."

"I always do," Rod said. "I'll see what I can learn."

"Don't forget I'm at the Bluegrass, if you come up with anything."

"Gotcha."

Clint left and went back to the hotel.

***

He knocked on McCall's door and Holly answered. On the way in both Wilkes an Olson gave him an all clear signal.

"How is he?" Clint asked.

"So relaxed he fell asleep."

"How did that happen?"

She smiled at him.

"I think you know."

"Did he tear any stitches?"

"No," she said, "I was gentle."

"Do you want a break?" Clint asked. "I can stay a while."

"I'm not tired," she said. "But I'm hungry, and Mad will be when he wakes up. How about a late lunch?"

"Okay," Clint said, "I'll go down and get some steaks."

"All the fixin's?"

"Yep," Clint said, "everything."

"Sounds good," Holly said. "So far this nursing job's payin' pretty good."

Chapter Thirty-Two

The steaks were certainly not the best Clint had ever had, but they were edible. They were better than what Holly usually ate. When McCall woke, they set him up on the bed so he could eat with one hand. Holly cut his meat for him, and while they ate, Clint told them about his afternoon.

"I never saw anyone in the Rusty Nail mad enough to kill Mad," Holly said. "But if anyone's gonna hear anythin' helpful, it's Rod. He's always got his ear to the ground."

"I figured," Clint said. "I'm going to relieve Wilkes and Olson so they can get something to eat."

"See you later, Clint," McCall said.

"How about bringin' back a bottle of champagne?" Holly asked.

"Done," Clint said. "I'll be about an hour."

***

Clint got Wilkes from the hall and took him down to the lobby. They were changing places from time to time.

"Go and eat," Clint said. "I'll cover. Take an hour."

"Sure," Wilkes said.

Olson and Wilkes went to the dining room. Clint decided to take up a position in the lobby so he could watch the door and do some thinking. He wondered how far Talbot Roper was getting in his investigation, and how Bat was recovering. Clint figured being shot from ambush like McCall, Bat was probably shot in the back. That's the safest way to kill someone like Bat, or McCall, or The Gunsmith. It was exactly the way Wild Bill Hickok was killed years ago. It didn't take courage to shoot someone in the back, it only took cowardice, and Kendall struck him as that kind of man. Or maybe it was just that he disliked him. He hoped Detective Pitkin was good at his job and would find out something useful. Clint had nothing to go on but his dislike of Kendall.

By the time Wilkes and Olson came out of the dining room Clint had an idea.

"Either one of you fellas know Griff Kendall?"

"I do," Wilkes said.

"Are you friends?"

"Hell, no," Wilkes said. "I wouldn't be friends with a snake like that."

"I'm thinking he might be my shooter," Clint said.

"Why would he do it?"

Clint explained the offer Kendall made to him, and how McCall spoke out against it.

"You think he wanted to shut McCall out?"

"That's the only thing I can think of," Clint said.

"Well," Wilkes said, "that's not somethin' Kendall would do himself. He'd hire it done."

"Who would he have hired?"

"Not me," Olson said.

"Or me," Wilkes said. "We're not killers."

"I wasn't insinuating that," Clint said. "Who do you think would do that kind of job?"

"There's a few men who would," Olson said, "but not us."

"Can you give me some names?" Clint asked.

"I don't wanna get anybody in trouble," Wilkes said.

"There are a few I don't mind mentioning," Olson said.

"Let's go over to the front desk so we can write this down."

"I'll go back upstairs," Wilkes said.

Olson and Clint went to the desk for some paper, and Olson wrote down three names and where to find them.

"Okay, Olson," Clint said. "Thanks."

Olson went over to the divan in the lobby that he had chosen to watch from.

Clint went back up to McCall's room and knocked, hoping he wasn't interrupting anything.

When Holly opened the door she looked a bit disheveled and breathless. In the bed McCall looked a little sweaty.

"Sorry to interrupt," Clint said, "but do you know any of these names, Mad?" He showed McCall the list of names.

"Yeah, I know two of 'em."

"Which two?"

"Arklow and Fleming."

"How do you know them?"

"They're troublemakers," McCall said. "I make it my business to know about men like them."

"And have you had trouble with either one?"

"No."

"And the third man?"

"Steele," McCall said. "I don't know him. Why are you askin' about all of them?"

"Olson gave me their names," Clint said. "I was looking for possible hired killers."

"Hired killers?" McCall said, "You think somebody got paid to shoot me?"

"You or me," Clint said. "I'm thinking about Kendall."

"Kendall," McCall said. "You think he was mad enough about bein' turned down that he'd hire a shooter?"

"Who knows?" Clint said. "There's no harm in asking."

"Are you gonna go and talk to these yahoos alone?" McCall asked. "Wait for me." He tossed the sheet back and started to get up, but stopped short when the pain hit him.

"That's enough, Mad," Holly said, stepping between then. "Stay in bed."

"One at a time shouldn't be a problem, Mad."

"No," McCall said, "probably not for you."

"He's the Gunsmith, Mad," Holly reminded him. "He can handle anythin'."

"Just make sure you watch your back," McCall said.

"I've had plenty of practice."

McCall pointed at the list.

"One of those places ain't friendly," McCall said.

"I'm going to treat them all that way," Clint said.

"Why don't you take Wilkes or Olson with you," McCall suggested.

"I want them here looking after you," Clint said, "and Holly."

"If you get yourself shot," McCall said, "I really am gonna get mad."

"I'm not getting shot," Clint promised him. "I don't want to get you mad."

Chapter Thirty-Three

The first man Clint tried was Trey Arklow. Olson told him he would find the man at a restaurant called The Dutch. It was in a section of town that, like McCall said, didn't look friendly. As Clint dismounted, he got hard looks from several men outside the place.

As he entered, he was confronted by a wide, hard looking man.

"Can I help ya?" he asked. "Table?"

"No, thanks, no table," Clint said, "I'm looking for a man named Arklow."

"Trey? What fer? He's workin'."

"Working? Here?"

"Whatamatta with here?" the man asked. "You got somethin' against my place?"

"No, nothing," Clint said. "I've just got too much business to take time to eat. What's Arklow do here?"

"He's my cook."

"Cook?"

"And not bad either. It surprised me, too."

"I thought he did a different kind of work," Clint said.

"With a gun?" The man shook his head. "He don't do that no more, not since he started to cook."

"Can I see him?"

The man looked around, saw mostly empty tables.

"Sure, he's in the kitchen," he said. "But don't keep him long. We got our supper rush startin' soon."

"I won't be long."

"Through there," the man said, pointing to a doorway.

He went through the door into a small, crowded kitchen. In the middle of the clutter was a tall man wearing a dirty apron. He was peeling potatoes.

"Hey, ya can't come in the kitchen," he said.

"The big man outside said I could."

"That's Dutch," the man said, "so I guess it's okay."

"Are you Trey Arklow?"

"I am," Arklow said. "Whataya need?"

"I was told you do a certain kind of job," Clint said. "I might need you."

"You mean you want somebody shot," Arklow said, "I don't do that no more. I traded in my gun for a stove."

"Is that on the level?"

"Oh yeah," Arklow said. "I like cookin'."

"But you used to kill people?" Clint asked.

"Not kill," Arklow said. "Anythin' but. But don't do any of that, no more."

"Then tell me," Clint said, "did a man named Kendall try to hire you to shoot something?"

"Kendall?" He shook his head. "Don't know 'im."

"Do you know who's for hire for what you used to do?"

"Lotsa fellas."

"You know a couple of men named Steele and Fleming?"

"Oh, sure, they'll put a bullet in anybody for a dollar," Arklow said. "But you look like you can do your own shootin'."

"I do," Clint said. "I'm looking for somebody who shot a friend of mine."

"Oh? Who was that?"

"Mad McCall."

"McCall?"

"You know him?"

"I've heard of him. He's a character. Who'd wanna shoot 'im?"

"That's what I'm trying to find out."

"Well," Arklow said, "far as I can see you're lookin' for the right fellas."

"Fleming and Steele."

"Either one of them," Arklow said, "but there are others. It'd take you a while to find 'em all and ask 'em."

"You were easy to find," Clint said.

"I ain't hidin' anymore," Arklow said. He spread his arms, potato peeler in one hand and spud in the other. "This is where I am." He went back to peeling. "Come and eat, some time."

Clint left without commenting.

Chapter Thirty-Four

Clint left The Dutch with second thoughts about looking for the others. Like Arklow said, they might not be as easy to find as he was if they were still in the business.

But if he didn't go looking for them, what would he do? He still had nobody in mind but Kendall.

He rode back to the Bluegrass, but kept the Tobiano out front in case he needed him. When he went into the lobby he saw Detective Pitkin talking with Olson.

"Detective Pitkin," he said, approaching, "Looking for me?"

"I was," Pitkin said. "I was just trying to find out what Mr. Olson was doing here. He said he was working for you."

"That's true."

Olson gave Pitkin a satisfied look.

"Then I guess I don't have to talk to him?"

"Why don't we go into the saloon?" Clint suggested.

This was the first time Clint had been in the hotel bar. He must have been pointed out to the bartender, who greeted him by now.

" 'afternoon, Mr. Adams. Drink?"

"Detective?" Clint said.

"Beer will do."

"Two beers," Clint said, "at that table."

"Sure thing."

Clint walked Pitkin over to a table in the rear of the room. The bartender followed with two beers.

"Thanks," Clint said.

"Mr. Lourde says all your meals and drinks should be charged to your room."

"That's fine."

He returned to the bar to see to other guests.

"What brings you here, Detective?"

"I had a talk with Mr. Kendall," Pitkin said.

"What did he have to say?"

"He was very upset that you sent me to question him," Pitkin said. "According to him he's only trying to build a business."

"How? By having Mad McCall shot?"

"He says he had nothing to do with that."

"You asked him?"

"I did, straight out," Pitkin said. "He denied it."

"Of course he would," Clint said. "You don't think he'd come right out and admit it, do you?"

"No, he wouldn't," the detective said, "but I thought he was on the level."

"Based on what?"

"Instinct."

"If you don't mind me asking, Detective, how long have you been with the Louisville police?"

"Two years."

"And you think you've sharpened your instincts in that time?"

"I came here from New York, Mr. Adams," Pitkin said. "I may not be thirty yet, but yes, I have sharpened my instincts."

"Sorry for questioning you, Detective," Clint said, "but I've got pretty good instincts, too, and mine are saying that Kendall's a little crooked."

"Maybe crooked in his business," Pitkin said, "but enough to have somebody killed?"

"To increase his sales? I think so."

"Himself?"

"No, but I wouldn't put it past him to hire it done."

"Hire who?"

"You could probably tell me that, Detective," Clint said. "I started talking to likely candidates today. But I found a man named Arklow working in a kitchen."

"Trey Arklow?" Pitkin said. "Yeah, he might've done it at one time, but not anymore."

"You know about his new career?"

"Yeah, he's a cook."

"That's for real?"

"Sure," Pitkin said. "I've tasted his cooking. It's not bad."

"At Dutch's?"

"Not the cleanest place in Louisville, but the food's not bad."

"You eat there often?"

"Once," Pitkin said, "just to see if Arklow was telling the truth."

"And he was?"

"Not a bad steak," Pitkin said.

"Okay," Clint said, "so you're convinced Kendall wasn't behind the shooting?"

"I'm convinced he didn't do it himself," Pitkin said. "I'll continue to keep my ears open."

"Thanks, Detective."

As Detective Pitkin left, Clint figured he had it covered with a bartender and a detective keeping their ears to the ground.

Olson came over and asked, "Anythin'?"

"No, not from Arklow or the detective."

"What about Steele and Fleming?"

"I haven't talked to them, yet, but I was thinking that it would probably be fruitless."

"What about Arklow?"

"He's a cook now, at Dutch's."

"Really? The food there is terrible."

"Apparently it's better since he put down his gun and picked up a spatula."

"Arklow's a cook? That's weird."

"I thought so, too, but he seemed to know his way around a potato peeler."

Chapter Thirty-Five

Clint decided to go ahead and find Fleming and Steele. If his instincts told him it wasn't them, maybe they would both give him the same name. Or maybe they would know Kendall.

He was told Fleming worked in a warehouse in a district of Louisville which was easy to locate. He wondered if, like Arklow, Fleming was another gunhand who changed professions.

When he entered, he was told that Fleming was working in the back, loading buckboards.

Clint found his way back there and saw several men loading buckboards. They all paused to look at him.

"I'm looking for a man named Fleming," Clint said.

A couple of the men pointed at another and went back to work.

"You're Fleming?" Clint asked.

A thickly built man in his forties turned to face him.

"That's right. What's on your mind?"

"Can we talk over here?"

Fleming nodded, and they walked to where they wouldn't be overheard.

"What is it?" Fleming asked. "I got work to do."

"That's what I want to talk to you about," Clint said, "A job."

"I got a job."

"I mean your other work."

Fleming frowned.

"What're you talkin' about?"

"You know," Clint said. "When a person has some-body they want . . . dealt with? They hire you."

A thoughtful look came over the man's face. He rubbed his jaw and said, "You're talkin' about somethin' I used to do. I don't do that no more."

"Seems like men in that line of work are turning to other careers these days."

Fleming's ruddy face broke into an ugly smile.

"You're talkin' about Arklow bein' a cook."

"Yes," Clint said, "I spoke with him."

"Whatever your job is, he turned ya down?"

"He did."

"Well, I'm turnin' ya down, too. I don't hurt people for money, no more."

"You used to hurt them, or kill them?"

"I didn't kill people," Fleming said, "I broke bones, that was it."

"You didn't hire your gun?"

"I never used a gun," Fleming said. "I don't like 'em. You look like you can use one."

"When I have to."

"Well, I never had to. I used these." He held out his hands, then allowed them to hang down at the end of his thick arms. Clint believed him.

"Did a man named Kendall ever try to hire you?"

"Kendall? Never heard of him."

"You know anybody still doing that kind of work?" Clint asked.

"I ain't givin' anybody up," Fleming said. "I'm mindin' my own business."

"Somebody shot Mad McCall. Any ideas?"

"Mad? "who'd shoot him?"

"That's my question."

"If I took a job to hurt McCall, I'd do it with my hands," Fleming said.

"He's a big man."

"I know," Fleming said. "It'd be interestin'."

"What about his gun?"

"I told you," Fleming said, "I never used a gun. McCall wouldn't shoot an unarmed man."

"Somebody shot him in the back," Clint said.

"I'd never do that," Fleming said.

Clint believed the man.

"Thanks, Mr. Fleming," Clint said.

"Just Fleming," the man said. "Nobody calls me Mister."

"Thanks."

"Sorry I can't help you," Fleming said. "I may not be in that business anymore, but I ain't about to talk about anybody else."

"That's okay," Clint said.

"It's gettin' late and I wanna finish my work."

Fleming went back to work, and Clint left the warehouse with a grudging respect for the man.

***

It looked like gunmen and hard men in this part of the country had more dignity than in the West. So far two of them weren't giving anybody else away. He wondered if it would make sense to talk to anyone else. Wilkes and Olson gave him names, but they didn't go as far as killing, and they didn't like men who did.

Fleming and Arklow claimed they didn't kill for money, either. On the other hand, nobody would admit to that. Not when it could come back and haunt them.

Chapter Thirty-Six

It was late when Clint got back to the Bluegrass. Olson and Wilkes had changed places, and Wilkes was seated on the divan in the lobby.

"How's everything?" Clint asked.

"That's what I was gonna ask you," Wilkes said. "Anythin'?"

"Nothing," Clint said. "Turns out some of the hired guns in town have changed jobs."

"Really? Arklow?"

"He's a cook now."

"A cook? Where?"

"A place called Dutch's."

"That place? The food's awful."

"Not anymore, apparently."

"I'll have to try it. Who else?"

"Fleming."

"What's he doin' now?"

"Stevedore."

"That's puttin' his broad back to good use. Did you see Steele?"

"No," Clint said, "but I'm starting to think this isn't such a good strategy."

"It may not be," Wilkes agreed.

"Tell me, how sure are you that Olson didn't do it?"

"Pretty sure," Wilkes said. "Are you gonna ask 'im the same question about me?"

"Probably."

"I would, just to be sure."

"Okay, thanks."

Clint went up to the second floor and saw Olson.

"Anythin'?" the man asked.

"Nothin,'" Clint said. "But I was wonderin' how sure are you that Wilkes wouldn't take that job?"

"Pretty sure," Olson said. "You ask him about me?"

"I did, and got the same answer."

"You're bein' thorough."

"That I am."

Clint went down the hall and knocked on McCall's door. When Holly opened it she said, "God, I'm glad you're here. Will you get him back in bed? He said he was going on out lookin' for you."

Clint entered the room and saw McCall struggling with his trousers.

"Okay," he said, "that's it. Get back in bed."

"There you are!" McCall said. "I was wonderin' what happened to you, what with the kind of yahoos you were lookin' for."

"Well, the yahoos I found are in a different business now."

He took McCall's pants away from him and helped him into bed. He took a look to make sure McCall hadn't opened his wound.

"Okay, settle back," Clint said. "Let Holly take care of you."

"Holly's been takin' real good care of me." He settled down beneath the sheet. "What's your next move gonna be?"

"To tell you the truth, I'm not sure," Clint said. "This is not my town, and I'm at kind of a loss about what to do next."

"Did you talk to Harry at the Stackhouse?"

"He's staying alert, and I've also got Detective Pitkin working on it."

"The only way you could do better was if you had me out there, too."

"Well, that's not happening. By the way, was Doc Fairlie in to see you?"

"He was here a couple of hours ago to check the wound and change the bandage," Holly said. "He said that so far I've been a good nurse."

McCall grinned.

"Doc said I look ten times better already."

"Thanks to Holly," Clint said.

"He don't know how much," McCall said.

"Let's not tell him," Clint suggested. "He might want to hire her full time."

"Not a chance," Holly said. "I have a full time job."

Clint turned to her.

"Isn't that something you'd like to get out of?"

"Why?" Holly asked. "I like it, and I'm very good at it. And I can make my own hours."

Clint shrugged.

"Just a thought."

"Are we gonna have dinner?" Holly asked.

"We had a late lunch," Clint reminded her.

"Then let's have an early dinner," she said. "This is the best food I've ever had."

Clint wondered if he should tell her to go and try the food at Dutch's.

"Right now I think I'll go to my room and wash up," he said, "then I'll go down to the dining room and get some food."

Holly linked her arm into his and walked him to the door.

"Steak?" she asked.

"That's what they do best," Clint said, not bothering to tell her it was the only thing they did for supper that was palatable.

Chapter Thirty-Seven

After he washed up Clint went down to the lobby, but before he could get to the dining room, he heard some commotion from the bar. He walked into the saloon, he saw the women of the WCTL standing at the bar. The older woman, Milly, was haranguing the bartender, who looked bewildered. The younger one, Gretchen, was looking dismayed. Clint decided to step in.

He walked to the bar, and since there weren't many people in the place, he was watched by all.

"Ah, Mr. Adams," the bartender greeted. "Can I get you—"

"Ignoring me will not make me go away, young man," Milly said, interrupting him. "And neither will helping this heathen sin."

The bartender did his best to ignore her despite her words.

"I'm sorry, sir," he said.

"That's all right," Clint said. "I've met these women before. Ladies, I think it'd be better if you tried to send your message somewhere else. This place never has very many sinners in it. Not like the other saloons, where they need your judgment more."

"I think Mr. Adams is right, Milly," Gretchen said. "They need us at the Shamrock."

"Yes, they do," the older woman said. "That place is crowded with sinners. Come, ladies."

She headed for the door, followed by the other ladies—all except Gretchen.

"Coming, Gretchen?" Milly asked.

"I'll be along," Gretchen said.

Milly sniffed loudly and led the other women out.

"Thank you, Mr. Adams," the bartender said. "Can I get you somethin'?"

"I don't think so" Clint said. "I'm going to walk this young lady out."

He took Gretchen's arm and walked her to the batwing doors. Outside he stopped and asked, "Why are you so much more understanding than the other ladies in your group?"

"I think that has to do with you, Mr. Adams."

"How do you mean?"

"Come with me and I'll show you."

This time Gretchen took his arm and led him away from the entrance, off the boardwalk and to the alley that ran alongside. They walked to the center of the alley, where there were a group of barrels set up.

"Why are we down here?" he asked.

"Let me show you," she said, again.

He was surprised when she took his hand with one of hers, raised her skirt with the other, revealing her lovely, alabaster thighs. She put his hands between them, where he discovered that she was wearing an undergarment with a slit in it. This enabled her to press his fingertips to her vagina, which was already slick with her moistness.

"Do you feel that?" she asked.

"Oh, yes, but—"

"I've been that wet since the first time we saw each other," she said, "and have been wearing that since the next morning, in the hopes I'd get a chance to do this."

He rubbed his finger until he found her wet clit, and her eyes rolled up in her head as she moaned.

"I don't understand," he said. "Isn't this sinning?"

She opened her eyes and said, "We all have our own little vices. Now will you please fuck me?"

Clint found the woman's actions and, in direct opposition to her appearance, to be incredibly exciting. He removed his gunbelt and set it aside on a barrel within easy reach, then dropped his trousers and lifted her up until she was seated on another barrel with her thighs spread. He stepped close and slid his incredibly hard cock up into her hot, wet depths, and she immediately wrapped those legs around his waist.

He began to pump in and out of her quickly, and she matched the rhythm of his hips, watching over his shoulder in case someone entered the alley.

"Please," she gasped, "faster and harder. We have to hurry."

"That's too bad," he said.

He increased speed and force and soon the barrel she was on was bouncing. Then she caught her breath and fought to keep from screaming, waiting until he exploded inside her before pushing him away, standing on her feet and smoothing her skirt down.

"Hurry," she said, "please, pull your trousers up."

He did as she asked, then strapped his gun back on while she patted her hair into place and caught her breath.

"I have to meet the others," she said.

"Where will you tell them you've been?"

"I'll think of something."

"All right."

He started to turn and she grabbed him.

"Wait." She wrapped her arms around his neck and kissed him soundly. "Thank you."

"No," he said, "thank *you*."

He went in for another kiss but she released him, turned and hurried from the alley.

Chapter Thirty-Eight

After their early supper, Clint took the plates down-stairs, and then spelled Wilkes and Olson in turn so they could eat. While sitting in the lobby he felt completely useless, and it wasn't a feeling he liked. If someone wanted to kill him in a smaller town than Louisville he would have put himself on display and waited for them to try again. He couldn't very well hang McCall out there as bait, and he still didn't know which of them was the intended target.

When Wilkes and Olson were back from their dinner, Clint went into the hotel bar and sat at a table giving the matter more thought over a beer.

He wished Bat Masterson had arrived already. That probably would have been all the help he needed. Or perhaps he would hear from Talbot Roper about who had shot Bat and that would help identify the shooter and who hired them. Having Bat and McCall shot in the back days apart was too much of a coincidence for someone like Clint, who didn't believe in them.

And then it suddenly occurred to Clint that there was someone he hadn't talked to, yet. He would make a point of correcting that the next morning.

***

In the morning Clint rose early so he could bring McCall and Holly some breakfast. Then he told Wilkes and Olson to eat separately, while he went out.

He fetched his Tobiano from the hotel livery and rode to the distillery owned by Ben Teller and, partially, Bat Masterson.

He tied his horse out front and went inside. The young man, Danny, was at the counter. He grinned when he saw Clint.

"You come back to order?" he asked. "Where's your friend?"

"My friend got shot. He's recuperating."

"That's terrible. Who shot 'im?"

"That's what I'm trying to find out. Is Mr. Teller around today?"

"He is, he's in the back. I'll tell 'im you're here."

"Tell him Clint Adams."

"Yes, sir."

Danny went through the door into the distillery, and returned leading an older man about Clint's age, but heavier.

"Mr. Adams?"

"That's right."

He stuck his hand out.

"Ben Teller," he said.

They shook hands.

"Mr. Masterson mentioned that you'd be comin'," Teller said. "Is he in town?"

"No, not yet. Let's go to your office."

"Sure, follow me."

They went down a hall to a door that led to a small office.

"Can I get you a drink?" Teller asked.

"No, thanks, I'm not a bourbon drinker. It would go to waste on me."

"I could get some beer."

"Maybe another time. Right now I want to talk."

"Okay," Teller said, sitting behind his desk. "Have a seat and talk."

Clint sat across from the man.

"How did you get involved with Bat, Mr. Teller?"

"He was looking at some of the breweries and distilleries in Louisville. He walked in here, introduced himself, and we talked."

"Did he taste anything?"

"Not the first time, but he came back. The second time he tasted some bourbon and my beer."

"Did he like them?"

"He must have," Teller said. "That's when we talked about becoming partners."

"Who brought it up? You or him?"

"Lemme think," Teller said. "I don't even remember."

"But you agreed?"

"Sure, we did."

"Did any money change hands?"

"No," Teller said, "Bat said he had an appointment in Denver but he'd come back."

"Did you talk to him about putting his name on your label?"

"We didn't get that far," Teller said, "but that ain't a bad idea."

"Do you know a man named Griff Kendall?"

"Sure, I know Griff. He owns a two-bit distillery on the other side of town."

"Is it considered bad to have your business there?"

"Well," Teller said, spreading his arms, "it ain't here." He placed his hands behind his head. "What's your interest in him?"

"It's he who has an interest in me," Clint said.

"Now that figures," Teller said. "Did he make you an offer?"

"He did," Clint said. "And I tasted his stock."

"And?"

"Like I told you, I don't drink bourbon, but I had my friend with me."

"And he drinks bourbon, right?"

"Yes, and he didn't like it."

"And the beer?"

Clint shook his head.

"And how did Griff take it?"

"Not well. I've seen him again since then, and it went even worse."

"Well, you don't wanna get involved with Griff Kendall."

"He's crooked?"

"He's small time," Teller said.

"What would he do to become successful?" Clint asked.

"Anythin'."

"Kill somebody?"

Teller hesitated, then said, "Not himself. Oh wait, you wanna know if he had your friend shot, don't you?"

"That's what I've been trying to find out," Clint said. "If he wanted it done, who would he use?"

"Any number of guys," Teller said.

"I've talked to a few and I can't find one."

"For enough money, any of them would do it," Teller said. "None of them would admit it."

"You got any names?"

Teller shook his head.

"I wouldn't wanna get anybody in trouble. I say keep an eye on Kendall. He'll make a mistake, eventually. He always does."

Clint stood up. "That may be the best advice I've gotten."

"Come on, I'll walk you out."

When they got to the front Teller asked, "Will you come back with Bat when he gets here?"

"After we talk," Clint said. "I didn't like being kept in the dark so long. I want to get the whole story from him."

"He'll tell you pretty much what I've told you."

"I just want to make sure this was really the only reason he asked me to meet him here."

"What other reason could there be?" Teller asked.

"With Bat? You never know."

Clint left, glad he had thought to stop in and meet Ben Teller.

Chapter Thirty-Nine

Clint's visit to Teller pretty much confirmed what he thought of Kendall. Now what he needed was to talk to someone about Teller. He decided that should be Detective Pitkin, so he rode to police headquarters.

***

Detective Pitkin just left, sir," the desk officer said.

"Do you know where he went?" Clint asked.

The young policeman hesitated.

"This is kind of important," Clint added.

"Well . . ." The young man leaned over the desk. "Go out the front door, turn right and walk down two streets. He might be in a place called The Dark Hole."

"That doesn't sound like a very cordial place."

"It is," the policeman said, "to law enforcement types. When you go in, just say you're lookin' for Detective Pitkin."

"I will. Thanks."

Clint left the building and followed the man's directions. He found The Dark Hole and it looked just like its name. Clint entered and was immediately the center of attention.

A man approached him and asked, "Can I help you, friend?"

"I'm looking for Detective Pitkin."

Before the man could reply, Pitkin appeared and said, "It's all right, Dave. I know Mr. Adams."

"Okay, Lieutenant."

"This way, Mr. Adams."

He led Clint to a private table in the back surrounded by a curtain of hanging beads.

"Have a seat. Beer?"

"Sure."

Pitkin waved and the bartender came over with two beers.

"What's on your mind, to bring you here to find me?" Pitkin asked.

"I had a conversation with a man named Ben Teller today," Clint said.

"I know Ben Teller," Pitkin said. "Do you think he was involved in the shooting of McCall?"

"No," Clint said, "I don't have any reason to, but he's supposed to have formed a partnership with Bat Masterson, and Bat's the reason I'm here."

"Masterson is in town?"

"No, I was supposed to meet him here, but he was shot while in Denver and he's going to be late."

"Was he badly hurt?"

"A telegram says no, but I won't know much until Bat does get here."

"Then why do you want me?"

"Teller gave me his opinion of Griff Kendall,'" Clint said, "and it pretty much matched mine. But now I want to hear your opinion of Teller."

"He's quite the opposite of Kendall," Pitkin said. "As far as I know, he's completely honest. If your friend Masterson wants to get into the distillery business, he could do worse."

"That's what I wanted to know," Clint said. He sipped his beer and set it down. "Thanks. I'll leave you to it."

Clint got up and left The Dark Hole, mounted his horse and rode back to the Bluegrass.

***

He took his horse to the hotel livery, and, instead of entering the lobby, he took the entrance to the hotel bar. It was largely for guests, so there weren't many customers there. Clint collected a beer from the bar and took it to a table. He was halfway finished with it when the desk clerk came in and approached his table.

"I thought you might want this quick, so I took a look in here, just in case."

The young man handed him a telegram.

"Thank you." He tipped the clerk, who went back to his desk.

The telegram was from Bat Masterson, who said he was on his way. It was sent that morning. He refolded it and put it in his shirt pocket. Maybe this whole thing was close to getting cleared up.

***

Clint finished his beer and went to his room, passing Olson in the hall. They exchanged nods. He paused outside McCall's room, but decided to let the man rest— or whatever he and Holly were doing.

He turned to his door, but stopped with his hand near the door knob. With Olson and Wilkes covering the lobby and the hall, there should have been no way for anyone to get into his room, and yet his instincts told him someone was in there.

With his right hand down by his gun, he inserted his key with his left, unlocked the door and swung it open, darting into the room.

"You make a heckuva entrance," Bat Masterson said to him.

Chapter Forty

"What the hell—" Clint said.

Bat was reclining on the bed, still wearing his gun and boots.

"I've got a man in the lobby and one in the hall. How the hell did you get in here?"

"There was nobody in the hall when I came up the back stairs," Bat said. "You need to get better men. But why do you have somebody on watch, anyway?"

"Someone took a shot at me and Mad McCall. He was hit. He's in this hotel recovering."

"Where?"

"Right across the hall."

"Let's close that door for now," Bat suggested.

Clint slammed it.

"Your telegram came today," Clint said.

"I had the telegraph operator hold back on it," Bat said. "I didn't want anyone knowing when I was coming."

Clint sat in the chair and stared at his friend.

"You want to tell me what's going on?" he asked.

"Let's compare notes."

Bat had been shot from ambush. The bullet hit him high on the left shoulder. Clint explained about McCall being shot in the back.

"Sounds like we both got lucky," Bat commented.

"Has Roper found the shooter?" Clint asked.

"Not when I left, but he's still looking."

"Bat, what is all this about. I talked with Ben Teller."

"What did he tell you?" Bat asked.

Clint related his conversation to Bat.

"I asked you to meet me here because I knew somebody was trying to use my name for their product."

"So you're not partners with Teller?"

"No," Bat said. "I won half his distillery in a poker game, but I agreed to sell it back to him when I got back from Denver. I had some business there I had to take care of before I could come back and settle this."

"Do you think you were shot because of this distillery thing?"

"Who knows why somebody takes it into their head to shoot at men like us. Why was McCall shot?"

Clint explained about Kendall and his distillery.

"Well, Mad knows good bourbon," Bat said. "It looks like right now we're in the same situation."

"The word I got is that Kendall's crooked, but Teller's on the level."

"That may be, but he's still a businessman looking for an angle."

"But would he have any reason to send someone to Denver to shoot you?"

"No, I don't think so," Bat said. "What about your man?"

"I'm sure he's behind it," Clint said. "He wanted Mad out of the way."

"And he thought having him shot would win you over?"

"His thinking is all wrong," Clint said, "only I have to prove it."

"I'll go with you," Bat said. "We can stop and set Teller straight on the way."

"Are you in shape for this?" Clint asked.

Bat slid off the bed, grimaced as he stood and said, "I'll be fine."

Chapter Forty-One

Clint and Bat decided to keep it between themselves that Bat was in town. Clint went to the dining room just before it closed and brought some food to the room for Bat. After that, they decided to share the bed.

In the morning Clint suggested they change their plan and tell McCall he was there. They crossed the hall and knocked. When Holly opened it Clint said, "Bat, this is Holly. She's acting as McCall's nurse. Holly, Bat Masterson."

"Nice to meet you, Mr. Masterson. Come in."

Bat entered and crossed the room to the bed.

"Hey, Mad."

"Bat." The two men shook hands.

"When did you get here?"

"Last night. How are you doin'?"

"Lousy."

"Hey!" Holly said.

"Except for my nursing. The Doc comes in and checks on me. He can take a look at you, too."

"I don't think I'm as bad as you are, Mad," Bat said.

"Mad, Bat and I are going downstairs for breakfast. When we're done, I'll bring some food up for you and

Holly. After we see that Wilkes and Olson are fed, Bat and I have some people to see."

"Kendall?" McCall asked.

"He's one of them," Clint said.

***

When everybody had been fed, Clint and Bat went to the livery. Bat got the same horse McCall had been using from the hostler.

"Where to first?" Bat asked, when they were mounted.

"I say Teller's distillery, so we can get that cleared up. Then we'll go and pressure Kendall and see if he can stand up to it."

"Okay," Clint said, "let's go."

***

They reined in their horses in front of Teller's distillery. When they entered, Danny looked up from papers on the counter.

"Mr. Adams . . . oh, Mr. Masterson! You're back."

"We're here to see Ben, Danny."

"He's in his office. I'll take you back there."

"We know the way," Clint said. To Bat he said, "Back here," and started down the hall.

They came to the office door and went in without knocking. Ben Teller looked up from his desk in surprise. When he recognized Bat, he didn't seem happy.

"Bat," he said, "Mr. Adams. This is a surprise." He looked at Bat. "Mr. Adams told me you'd been shot."

"I was, in Denver," Bat said.

"I hope you're okay," Teller said.

"I'll live. Do you have what we talked about?"

"No, not yet."

"Why'd you tell Clint we were partners?"

"We are . . . until I can buy your half back. That was our agreement. But I thought maybe when you came back, you'd change your mind."

"I haven't," Bat said. He looked at Clint. "I won half the business in a poker game, but agreed to sell it back when he found an investor."

"And I haven't found one, yet."

"If you were hoping Bat would change his mind, you must not have been looking too hard."

"It's hard to find somebody," Teller said, "especially with a snake like Griff Kendall also lookin'. He gives us all a bad name."

"You're doing a good job of that yourself by lying," Clint said.

"I wasn't lyin' . . . not exactly. I was just hopin' I could convince Bat when he got back. Or even you, when we met."

"I'm afraid neither of us is interested in the distillery business," Bat said.

"What about with your picture on the label?" Teller asked.

"Especially not with our picture on the label," Clint said.

Teller sat back, shoulders slumped.

"This business looks pretty healthy, Teller," Clint said.

"I want it to be more successful," Teller said.

"Well," Clint said, "you're going to have to do it without us."

"I know that, now."

"Do you have any possible investors?" Bat asked.

"I might have a couple, but . . ."

"But you were waiting for me to get back," Bat finished.

"I guess . . ."

"Well, I'm back," Bat said. "See what you can do about getting me that money."

"Yeah, okay."

"I'll probably be here a few more days," Bat said. "At the Bluegrass."

"All right."

As Clint and Bat started out the door Teller called out, "How about a poker game?"

Chapter Forty-Two

In front of the distillery they paused before mounting up.

"We didn't ask him about your shooting," Clint said.

"I don't think he had anything to do with shooting me," Bat said. "If he wanted that, why wait til I'm in Denver. He could've had it done here. Besides, I don't see any reason for it. His business is solid enough."

"Maybe the same can't be said for Griff Kendall," Clint said.

"Then let's try him," Bat said.

"You feeling up to it?" Clint asked.

"I'm fine," Bat said. "Let's see what we can squeeze out of this Kendall.'

They mounted up and started away when the door to the distillery opened and Danny came rushing out. Clint and Bat weren't right in front of the door, and Danny ran the other way, so he didn't see them.

"Where do you think he's going?" Clint asked.

"Maybe we should find out," Bat suggested.

They dismounted and started off following Danny on foot.

***

Danny was in a hurry to get wherever he was going. He never looked over his shoulder.

"He's sure in a rush," Bat said.

"The question is, is he on his own, or did Teller send him somewhere?"

"We're gonna find that out."

Danny only went a block before he waved down a horse drawn cab.

"Great," Clint said. "We should've kept our horses."

"You run back and get yours. I'll follow as soon as I can. I'm not ready for any running."

"Okay," Clint said, "I'll see you back at the hotel."

He turned and ran back to where he had left his To-biano, mounted up and gave the horse his heels. He hoped he would be able to catch up to the cab and follow it.

As he rode past Bat, his friend pointed in the direction Danny's cab had gone. Clint waved back and kept going at a gallop. After a few streets he spotted the cab, slowed down and stayed in easy view.

It didn't take Clint long to realize where they were going. Eventually, the cab pulled up in front of Griff Kendall's distillery. Danny got out of the cab, ran up the steps and entered.

Clint went past the distillery, tied his horse off about half a block away, then walked back. He decided to walk right in and see what he interrupted. But the door was locked, which meant somebody must have let Danny in. He tried to force the door, but it was solid. His only way in would be to knock. He could have circled the building and looked for another way in, but that would take too long. He wanted to get inside while Danny was still there. He wanted to know if Danny had gone there on his own, or been sent by Teller. If the young man had gone of his own accord, then maybe he was working both sides. If Teller sent him, then maybe Teller and Kendall were working together. That was a possibility that had never occurred to him.

Clint pounded his fist on the door and waited. He was about to knock again when the door opened and Griff Kendall glared at him.

"What do you want?" the man demanded.

"Sorry to interrupt the two of you."

"What do you mean, the two of us?"

"You and Danny."

"I don't know wha—"

"Come on, Kendall," Clint said. "I followed Danny here from Ben Teller's place."

Kendall hesitated, then said, "All right, you might as well come in."

Clint followed Kendall to his office. As they entered Danny turned and looked alarmed.

"Why'd you bring 'im back here?" the young man demanded. "Now he knows."

"He knew when he got here," Kendall said. "He followed you. You were careless." The man turned to Clint. "What do you want?"

"I want to know how long you and Ben Teller have been working together."

"What?" Kendall blurted before he could think. "I— well—"

"Never mind," Clint said. "That answered my question. You're not working together. Danny's working for both of you. Only Teller doesn't know it."

"I'm just tryin' to make a livin'!" Danny said. "What's wrong with that?"

"I don't know," Clint said. "Maybe I'll ask Teller."

"No! Don't! He'll fire me."

"So what? If he does, you'll still work here."

"No he won't."

"Griff!" Danny said, alarmed.

"He's only workin' for me so he can tell me what's goin' on at Teller's. If he doesn't work there, he won't work anywhere."

"No," Danny said, "I can keep him from firin' me. You'll see!"

Danny ran out.

Chapter Forty-Three

"Now what?" Clint asked Kendall.

"Whatayou mean?"

"You've lost your spy."

Kendall went around behind his desk and sat.

"You've got it wrong," he said. "Danny came to me and offered his services."

"Why did he think you'd accept?"

"Teller and me, we don't like each other. He thinks he's better than me."

"What did Danny offer you?"

"He told me Teller was going to be working with Bat Masterson."

"And what did that mean to you?"

"That his product would probably outsell mine."

"So you had somebody shoot Masterson in Denver?"

"What? Are you crazy? Why would I send somebody to Denver? You know what that would've cost me?"

"What did it cost you to have Mad McCall shot here?" Clint asked.

"That again? Adams, I didn't have anybody shoot anybody. I want to sell my product, but not bad enough to kill anybody. You keep lookin' all you want, you're not gonna find a soul in Louisville who took money from me to shoot anybody."

"So when you heard about Masterson, did that give you the idea to approach me?"

"It did, but that was later, after I heard that the Gunsmith was in town. I mean, why not? If Teller was gonna have Bat Masterson, why not one up him and get the Gunsmith?"

"Well, neither one of you got your man."

As Clint started to leave Kendall stood up.

"Why not look at Ben Teller?"

"What reason would Teller have? They're partners."

"Temporarily," Kendall said. "According to Danny, Masterson wanted Teller to buy him out. By killin' him, he saves money."

"Yeah, but having him killed costs money."

"Then what you need to find out is, which is cheaper."

Clint considered Kendall's words, and then left.

***

When Clint returned to the Bluegrass, Bat was there in the bar. Clint got two beers and joined him at his table.

"So where'd he go?"

"Over to Griff Kendall's distillery."

"Did Teller send 'im?"

"Not according to Kendall," Clint said. "He says Danny came to him and has been working for him."

"Why?"

"Danny says he's just trying to make a living; Kendall and Teller don't like each other. They're each trying to stay ahead of the other one."

"Enough to have somebody shot?"

"Kendall says no. He especially wouldn't pay to send somebody to Denver to do the job."

"And McCall?"

"He still says no," Clint said. "I guess that leaves us stuck where we were."

"Not exactly."

"What do you mean?"

"When I got back, the desk clerk gave me this for you." Bat handed him a telegram.

"Roper?" Clint asked.

"Yes. He found my shooter. Just some two-bit gunman who recognized me and decided to take a shot."

"So it's a coincidence and has nothing to do with Louisville."

"I knew you'd hate that."

"I do hate coincidences, but at least it answers one question."

"Which leaves only one left," Bat said.

"Who shot McCall?" Clint said.

Chapter Forty-Four

Clint and Bat stared into their beers for a few minutes, and then Clint said, "Something just occurred to me."

"Good, we need somethin'," Bat said. "What is it?"

"I had a man in the lobby and a man in the hall," Clint said. "How did you get into the room?"

"I stopped at the desk, the clerk recognized my name and gave me a key."

"That's how you got it," Clint said, "but how were you able to get in without being seen?"

"I thought it would be better to take the back stairs."

"Olson or Wilkes should've been in the hall."

"I didn't see anybody when I came up," Clint said.

"You saw one in the lobby, right?"

"Yeah, he was kinda obvious."

"Clean-shaven or bearded?"

"Clean-shaven."

"That would be Wilkes," Clint said. "Where the hell was Olson?"

"Beats me."

Clint slid his chair back.

"I'm going to find out."

"I'll come with you."

***

Clint first stopped by Wilkes.

"Have you seen Olson all day?" he asked.

"As a matter of fact, I ain't seen him since this mornin' . . . an' I thought we wuz gonna switch places. What gives?"

"I'm going to find out right now."

When they reached the bottom of the stairs Clint asked, "You want to wait here instead of going up the stairs."

"Just go," Bat said, impatiently. "I can walk up a flight of stairs."

They both went up and found the hall empty.

"Where is he?" Bat asked.

"He's supposed to be here, and he wasn't when you got here, and he's not now. What the hell. I thought I could rely on him."

"And if you can't, maybe he's not who you thought he was. Who recommended him to you?"

"McCall sent me to Harry, the bartender at the Stackhouse, and he introduced me to both Wilkes and Olson."

"Well, there's a sure way to find out if he's reliable."

"McCall!" Clint snapped.

They both rushed down the hall to McCall's door, which was locked. Clint knocked, but Holly didn't answer. Then there were odd sounds from inside.

"Stand aside," Clint said to Bat.

Bat moved, and Clint backed away, then kicked out. His heel struck the door, which slammed open. He and Bat rushed in, gun hands ready, but had to stop short.

Olson was standing behind Holly with his arm around her neck, his gun out.

"Stand easy, Clint," he said.

"Who are you working for, Olson?" Clint asked. "Teller or Kendall?"

"What? Gee, neither of those two. Harry got me in here to take care of McCall for him."

"Harry?" McCall said, from the bed.

"McCall sent me to Harry," Clint said.

"That's right," Olson said, "and Harry took advantage of the situation to rid himself of McCall."

"I thought they were friends, "Clint said.

"We were never friends," McCall said. "I just thought Harry could help you find somebody reliable."

Olson laughed.

"Oh, Harry is definitely not McCall's friend. He just wanted me to finish the job somebody else started."

"Wait a minute," Clint said. "You didn't shoot McCall?"

"Me? Naw, I came in after."

"Why'd you decide to make a move now?" Clint asked.

"I heard Masterson was in town. I thought I'd better get it over with and light out."

"So what are you going to do now?" Bat asked. "You can't get away."

"I think we're gonna hafta see about that," Olson said, tightening his hold on Holly.

"Let her breathe, Olson," Clint said.

"Oh, sure," Olson said, easing up. "She's not the one I'm after, anyway," He pushed Holly so that she rammed into Clint, then turned his gun toward McCall.

"Don't, Olson!" Bat shouted. "You kill him, then you die. You don't want that."

"No," Olson said, "I want McCall to walk out with me."

"He can't!" Holly said.

"You heard the nurse," Clint said. "McCall can't walk."

"I'd hate to shoot a man who's lyin' in bed, and then walk out with Holly."

"You're not going anywhere, Olson," Clint said.

"If you kill me after I kill McCall, I still got my job done."

"What do you have against McCall, Olson?" Clint asked.

"Nothin'," the big man said. "It's just a job."

"Well," Clint said, "Killing you after you've killed McCall wouldn't be doing my job."

"Don't try it—" Olson started, but before he could finish Clint drew and fired.

Chapter Forty-Five

Clint entered the Stackhouse Saloon with Bat Masterson and they both went to the bar.

"Hey, Mr. Adams," Harry greeted. "What can I getcha?"

"Two beers, Harry."

"Comin' up."

Harry drew two cold ones and brought them over.

"What's goin' on?" Harry asked. "How's McCall?"

"He's fine," Clint said, "in spite of your efforts."

"My efforts? Whataya talkin' about?"

"Olson gave you away, right before I shot him last night."

Harry contrived to look confused, but he just looked nervous.

"I don't know what—"

"Don't worry, Harry," Clint said. "This is Bat Masterson."

"What? Bat? Now look—"

"Relax," Clint said, "Neither of us is going to do anything to you. Mad McCall wants to take care of you himself."

"Mad knows?"

"Oh yeah," Clint said. "He sent us here to let you know he'll be seeing you as soon as he gets on his feet."

"Mr. Adams, you can't let 'im —"

"Wrong, Harry" Clint said, "I can't stop him."

Clint and Bat left without touching their beer.

***

Holly opened the door for them.

"You give him the message?" McCall called from the bed.

"We gave it to him," Clint said. "If he's smart he's already left town."

"Why'd you let him go, Mad?" Bat asked.

"Oh, don't worry, I'll find 'im," McCall said. "I just need a few more days here to get back to full strength."

"You got 'em," Clint said. "When the Doc lets you go, we'll have a good meal."

At that point Clint heard someone knocking on his door across the hall. He opened McCall's door and saw Detective Pitkin standing there.

"Detective."

Pitkin turned.

"Ah, there you are, Mr. Adams," he said. "Is McCall in there?"

"He is," Clint said. "Come on in."

Pitkin entered and Clint closed the door. Holly looked the man up and down, and Clint made the introductions.

"Bat Masterson, Holly," Clint said, "this is Detective Pitkin."

"Hello," Bat said, and Holly smiled.

"And you know McCall."

"We've met," Pitkin said. "I wanted to tell you we found who shot you."

"Who was it?" McCall asked.

"A man named Robbins, Sam Robbins."

McCall frowned.

"Don't know 'im."

"He knows you," Pitkin said. "He said he had a run in with you a few months ago, and you roughed him up. He saw you on the street and decided to get back at you."

"How'd you find him?" Clint asked.

"I didn't. He turned himself in. Apparently, he felt bad about what he did. I think maybe he doesn't want McCall to kill him." Pitkin gave McCall a hard stare. "I don't want you to, either."

"Sure," McCall said. "I don't know 'im, anyway, and probably wouldn't be able to find 'im."

Pitkin turned to Clint.

"Walk me down?"

"Sure." To Bat he said, "Be right back."

188

They stepped out of the room and started down.

"Where are your men?" Pitkin asked.

"That's a story," Clint said, and started talking . . .

***

Clint came back to McCall's room.

"You explain it to him?" McCall asked.

"Yeah, told him we took Olson to an undertaker."

"He accepted that?" Bat asked.

"I told him I had no choice," Clint said. "He said he hopes Harry doesn't show up dead."

"Don't worry," McCall said. "Nobody's gonna find Harry."

Clint also knew that, thanks to Mad McCall, nobody would ever see Sam Robbins again. McCall would do whatever he had to do to find both men.

As they reached the lobby Clint said, "Wait a minute. Why was it you asked me to come to Louisville to meet you in the first place? You were going to tell me what when you got here."

"Yes, I was, but I was hoping you'd forget about it."

Clint stopped walking and insisted, "What was it?"

"Well . . . I did have it in my head to keep half the brewery, but I thought I needed the advice of somebody who knew me well. Then I had to go to Denver, I had committed to referee a fight. While there, I started having second thoughts, but I'd already asked you to meet me there. I figured you were already there, or on the way."

"And now you've decided you don't want it."

"If Teller and Kendall are a sample of people in the distillery business, not a chance."

"So what now?" Clint asked.

"Well, there's a big poker game over in Lexington."

"That sounds more like you. We better get you a room, Bat," Clint said.

Clint and Bat started walking again.

"I guess the whole thing—my shooting and McCall's—were coincidences that had nothing to do with each other, or with a distillery," Bat said, as they walked to the front desk.

"I hate to say it," Clint said, "but looks like you might be right."

Upcoming New Release!

THE GUNSMITH

CHANTEUSE FROM THE EAST
BOOK 482

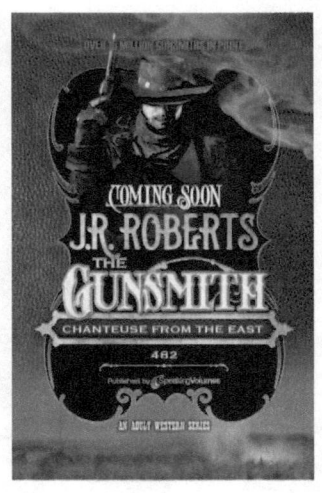

Clarice DuPont is a famous songstress from the east whose manager convinces her it's time to go west. She does have second thoughts, however, which prompts him to find an escort/bodyguard for her. He decides to ask Clint Adams who finds the request different enough to consider…

For more information
visit:

Now Available!

LADY GUNSMITH
BOOKS 1 - 10

For more information
visit:

Now Available!

AWARD-WINNING AUTHOR
ROBERT J. RANDISI (J.R. ROBERTS)

For more information
visit: www.SpeakingVolumes.us

Now Available!

TALBOT ROPER NOVELS
ROBERT J. RANDISI

For more information
visit: www.SpeakingVolumes.us